W9-CFL-619

RANDOM
HOUSE
LARGE
PRINT

No One
is Talking
About This

No One
is Talking
About This

Patricia
Lockwood

RANDOM HOUSE
LARGE PRINT

This is a work of fiction. Names, characters, places, and incidents either are the product of the author's imagination or are used fictitiously, and any resemblance to actual persons, living or dead, businesses, companies, events, or locales is entirely coincidental.

Copyright © 2021 by Patricia Lockwood

Penguin supports copyright. Copyright fuels creativity, encourages diverse voices, promotes free speech, and creates a vibrant culture. Thank you for buying an authorized edition of this book and for complying with copyright laws by not reproducing, scanning, or distributing any part of it in any form without permission. You are supporting writers and allowing Penguin to continue to publish books for every reader.

All rights reserved.

Published in the United States of America by Random House Large Print in association with Riverhead Books, an imprint of Penguin Random House LLC.

Cover design: Lauren Peters-Collaer
Cover image: Busà Photography / Moment / Getty Images

The Library of Congress has established a Cataloging-in-Publication record for this title.

ISBN: 978-0-593-39571-4

www.penguinrandomhouse.com/
large-print-format-books

FIRST LARGE PRINT EDITION

Printed in the United States of America

This Large Print edition published in accord with the standards of the N.A.V.H.

for Lena, who was a bell

There will be!

People!

On the sun!

Soon!

VLADIMIR MAYAKOVSKY,
"I and Napoleon"

Part One

She opened the portal, and the mind met her more than halfway. Inside, it was tropical and snowing, and the first flake of the blizzard of everything landed on her tongue and melted.

Close-ups of nail art, a pebble from outer space, a tarantula's compound eyes, a storm like canned peaches on the surface of Jupiter, Van Gogh's **The Potato Eaters**, a chihuahua perched on a man's erection, a garage door spray-painted with the words STOP! DON'T EMAIL MY WIFE!

Why did the portal feel so private, when you only entered it when you needed to be everywhere?

■ ■ ■

She felt along the solid green marble of the day for the hairline crack that might let her out. This could not be forced. Outside, the air hung swagged and the clouds sat in piles of couch stuffing, and in the south of the sky there was a tender spot, where a rainbow wanted to happen.

Then three sips of coffee, and a window opened.

■ ■ ■

I'm convinced the world is getting too full lol, her brother texted her, the one who obliterated himself at the end of every day with a personal comet called Fireball.

■ ■ ■

Capitalism! It was important to hate it, even though it was how you got money. Slowly, slowly, she found herself moving toward a position so philosophical even Jesus couldn't have held it: that she must hate capitalism while at the same time loving film montages set in department stores.

■ ■ ■

Politics! The trouble was that they had a dictator now, which, according to some people (white), they had never had before, and according to other people (everyone else), they had only ever been having, constantly, since the beginning of the world. Her stupidity panicked her, as well as the way her voice now sounded when she talked to people who hadn't stopped being stupid yet.

The problem was that the dictator was very funny, which had maybe always been true of all dictators. Absurdism, she thought. Suddenly all those Russian novels where a man turns into a teaspoonful of blackberry jam at a country house began to make sense.

■ ■ ■

What had the beautiful thought been, the bright profundity she had roused herself to write down? She opened her notebook with the sense of anticipation she always felt on such occasions—perhaps this would finally be it, the one they would chisel on her gravestone. It read:

chuck e cheese can munch a hole in my you-know-what

■ ■ ■

After you died, she thought as she carefully washed her legs under the fine needles of water, for she had recently learned that some people didn't, you would see a little pie chart that told you how much of your life had been spent in the shower arguing with people you had never met. Oh but like that was somehow less worthy than spending your time carefully monitoring the thickness of beaver houses for signs of the severity of the coming winter?

■ ■ ■

Was she **stimming**? She feared very much that she was.

■ ■ ■

Things that were always there:

The sun.

Her body, and the barest riffling at the roots of her hair.

___

An almost music in the air, unarranged and primary and swirling, like yarns laid out in their colors waiting.

The theme song of a childhood show where mannequins came to life at night in a department store.

Anonymous History Channel footage of gray millions on the march, shark-snouted airplanes, silk deployments of missiles, mushroom clouds.

An episode of **True Life** about a girl who liked to oil herself up, get into a pot with assorted vegetables, and pretend that cannibals were going to eat her. Sexually.

The almost-formed unthought, Is there a bug on me???

A great shame about all of it, all of it.

■ ■ ■

Where had the old tyranny gone, the tyranny of husband over wife? She suspected most of it had been channeled into weird ideas about supplements, whether or not vinyl sounded "warmer," and which coffee-makers were nothing but **a shit in the mouth of the coffee christ**. "A hundred years ago you would have been mining coal and had fourteen children all named Jane," she often marveled, as she watched a man stab a finger at his wife in front of the Keurig display. "Two hundred years ago, you might have been in a coffee shop in Göttingen, shaking the daily paper, hashing out the questions of the day—and I would be shaking out sheets from the windows, not knowing how to read." But didn't tyranny always feel like the hand of the way things were?

■ ■ ■

It was a mistake to believe that other people were not living as deeply as you were. Besides, you were not even living that deeply.

■ ■ ■

The amount of eavesdropping that was going on was enormous, and the implications not yet known. Other people's diaries streamed around her. Should she be listening, for instance, to the conversations of teenagers? Should she follow with such avidity the compliments that rural sheriffs paid to porn stars, not realizing that other people could see them? What about the thread of women all realizing they had the exact same scar on their knee? "I have that scar too!" a white woman piped up, but was swiftly and efficiently shut down, because it was not the same, she had interrupted an usness, the world in which she got that scar was not the same.

■ ■ ■

She lay every morning under an avalanche of details, blissed, pictures of breakfasts in Patagonia, a girl applying her foundation with a hard-boiled egg, a shiba inu in Japan leaping from paw to paw to greet its owner, ghostly pale women posting pictures of their bruises—the world pressing closer and closer, the spiderweb of human connection grown so thick it was almost a shimmering and solid silk, and the day still not opening to her. What did it mean that she was allowed to see this?

If she began to bite her lower lip, as she nearly always did after the milk and civet-cat bitterness of her morning coffee, she went into the bathroom with the ivy growing out its bangs outside the window and very carefully painted her mouth a definite, rich, top-of-the-piano red—as if she had an underground club to be at later that night, where she would go as bare as a missing sequin, where she would distill the whole sunset cloud of human feeling to a six-word lyric.

■ ■ ■

Something in the back of her head hurt. It was her new class consciousness.

■ ■ ■

Every day their attention must turn, like the shine on a school of fish, all at once, toward a new person to hate. Sometimes the subject was a war criminal, but other times it was someone who made a heinous substitution in guacamole. It was not so much the hatred she was interested in as the swift attenuation, as if their collective blood had made a decision. As if they were a species that released puffs of poison, or black ink in a cloud on the ocean floor. I mean, have you read that article about octopus intelligence? Have you read how octopuses are marching out of the sea and onto dry land, in slick and obedient armies?

■ ■ ■

"Ahahaha!" she yelled, the new and funnier way to laugh, as she watched footage of bodies being flung from a carnival ride at the Ohio State Fair. Their trajectories through the air were pure arcs of joy, T-shirts turned liquid on them, just look what the flesh could do when it gave in, right down to the surrendering snap of the . . .

"What's so hilarious," said her husband, resting sideways on his chair with his bladelike shins dangling over one arm, but by then she had scrolled down the rest of the thread and seen that someone was dead, and five others hanging half in and half out of the world. "Oh God!" she said as she realized. "Oh Christ, no, oh God!"

■ ■ ■

At nine o'clock every night she gave up her mind. Renounced it, like a belief. Abdicated it, like a throne, all for love. She went to the freezer and opened that fresh air on her face and put fingerprints in the frost on the neck of a bottle and poured something into a glass that was very very clear. And then she was happy, though she worried every night, as you never do with knowledge, whether there would be enough.

■ ■ ■

Inside the portal, a man who three years ago only ever posted things like "I'm a retard with butt aids" was now exhorting people to open their eyes to the power of socialism, which suddenly did seem the only way.

■ ■ ■

Her pronoun, which she had never felt particularly close to, traveled farther and farther away from her in the portal, swooping through landscapes of **us** and **him** and **we** and **them**. Occasionally it flew back to light on her shoulder, like a parrot who repeated everything she said but otherwise had nothing to do with her, who in fact had been left to her by some old weird aunt, who on her deathbed had simply barked, "Deal with it!"

Mostly, though, it passed into **you**, **you**, **you**, **you**, until she had no idea where she ended and the rest of the crowd began.

■ ■ ■

There was an iconic photograph, crisp in its nurse's uniform, of a woman being bent backward and kissed by a soldier on V-Day. We had seen it all our lives, and thought we understood the particular firework it captured—and now the woman had risen from history to tell everyone that she didn't know the man at all, that in fact she had been frightened throughout the whole encounter. And only then did the hummingbird of her left hand, the uncanny twist of her spine, the grip of the soldier's elbow on her neck become apparent. "I had never seen him before in my life," the woman said, and there he was in the picture, there he was in our minds, clutching her like victory, never letting her go.

■ ■ ■

Of course it was always the people who called themselves enlightened who stole the most. Who picked up the slang the earliest. To show—what? That they were not like the others? That they knew what was worth stealing? They were the guiltiest too. But guilt was not worth anything.

■ ■ ■

There was a new toy. Everyone was making fun of it, but then it was said to be designed for autistic people, and then no one made fun of it anymore, but made fun of the people who were making fun of it previously. Then someone else discovered a stone version from a million years ago in some museum, and this seemed to prove something. Then the origin of the toy was revealed to have something to do with Israel and Palestine, and so everyone made a pact never to speak of it again. And all of this happened in the space of like four days.

■ ■ ■

She opened the portal. "Are we all just going to keep doing this till we die?" people were asking each other, as other days they asked each other, "Are we in hell?" Not hell, she thought, but some fluorescent room with eternally outdated magazines where they waited to enter the memory of history, paging through a copy of **Louisiana Parent** or **Horse Illustrated**.

■ ■ ■

It was in this place where we were on the verge of losing our bodies that bodies became the most important, it was in this place of the great melting that it became important whether you called it **pop** or **soda** growing up, or whether your mother cooked with garlic salt or the real chopped cloves, or whether you had actual art on your walls or posed pictures of your family sitting on logs in front of fake backdrops, or whether you had that one Tupperware stained completely orange. You were zoomed in on the grain, you were out in space, it was the brotherhood of man, and in some ways you had never been flung further from each other. You zoomed in and zoomed in on that warm grain until it looked like the coldness of the moon.

■ ■ ■

"What are you doing?" her husband asked softly, tentatively, repeating his question until she shifted her blank gaze up to him. What was she **doing**? Couldn't he see her arms all full of the sapphires of the instant? Didn't he realize that a male feminist had posted a picture of his **nipple** that day?

■ ■ ■

She had become famous for a post that said simply, **Can a dog be twins?** That was it. Can a dog be twins? It had recently reached the stage of penetration where teens posted the cry-face emoji at her. They were in high school. They were going to remember "Can a dog be twins?" instead of the date of the Treaty of Versailles, which, let's face it, she didn't know either.

■ ■ ■

This had raised her to a certain airy prominence. All around the world, she was invited to speak from what felt like a cloudbank, about the new communication, the new slipstream of information. She sat onstage next to men who were better known by their usernames and women who drew their eyebrows on so hard that they looked insane, and tried to explain why it was objectively funnier to spell it **sneazing.** This did not feel like real life, exactly, but nowadays what did?

■ ■ ■

In Australia, where she was inexplicably popular, she sat onstage under melting lights with a fellow internet expert who bore the facial satisfaction of being Canadian and whose hair was visibly gelled with $32 gel.

He spoke well and cogently on a variety of subjects, but the pants he was wearing were Cyber Pants, the sort of pants we wore back when we believed we had to skateboard through the internet. He also wore rave goggles at all times, so as to protect himself from the blinding light of cyber, which came from a sun that he carried with him, directly in his line of vision, which was the star of the future set in the old bone socket of the sky.

"**Sneazing** is funnier, right?" she asked him.

"No question," he answered. "**Sneazing** all the way."

■ ■ ■

During these appearances there entered into her body what she thought of as a demon of performance, an absolutely intact personality that she had no access to in ordinary times. It was not just inside her, but spilled a little beyond; it struck huge gestures off her body like sparks from a flint. Always when she watched the performances afterward she was aghast. Who is that woman? Who told her she could talk to people that way?

■ ■ ■

"The problem!" She sounded militant, like a lesser-known suffragette. A foreign gnat was stuck in her mascara, and her mouth tasted of the minutely different preparation of coffee that Australians found superior to the latte. The audience looked at her encouragingly. "The problem is that we're rapidly approaching the point where all our dirty talk is going to include sentences like **Fuck up my dopamine, Website!**"

■ ■ ■

Why had she elected to live so completely in the portal? It had something to do, she knew, with Child Chained Up in the Yard. Her great-grandmother, an imaginary invalid, had kept her firstborn son chained up to a stake in the front yard so she could always see what he was doing through the window. She would have preferred a different maternal lineage—aviatrixes, jazz kittens, international spies would all have been preferable—but Child Chained Up in the Yard is what she had gotten, and it would not let her go.

■ ■ ■

Every country seemed to have a paper called **The Globe**. She picked them up wherever she went, laying her loonies and her pounds and her kroners down on counters, but often abandoned them halfway through for the immediacy of the portal. For as long as she read the news, line by line and minute by minute, she had some say in what happened, didn't she? She had to have some say in what happened, even if it was only WHAT?

Even if it was only HEY!

■ ■ ■

It was a place where she knew what was going to happen, it was a place where she would always choose the right side, where the failure was in history and not herself, where she did not read the wrong writers, was not seized with surges of enthusiasm for the wrong leaders, did not eat the wrong animals, cheer at bullfights, call little kids Pussy as a nickname, believe in fairies or mediums or spirit photography, blood purity or manifest destiny or night air, did not lobotomize her daughters or send her sons to war, where she was not subject to the swells and currents and storms of the mind of the time—which could not be escaped except through genius, and even then you probably beat your wife, abandoned your children, pinched the rumps of your maids, had maids at all. She had seen the century spin to its conclusion and she knew how it all turned out. Everything had been decided by a sky in long black judge robes, and she floated as the head at the top of it and saw everything, everything, backward, backward, and turned away in fright from her own bright day.

■ ■ ■

"Colonialism," she hissed at a beautiful column, while the tour guide looked at her with concern.

Every fiber in her being strained. She was trying to hate the police.

"Start small and work your way up," her therapist suggested. "Start by hating Officer Big Mac, a class traitor who is keeping the other residents of McDonaldland from getting the sandwiches that they need, and who when the revolution comes will have the burger of his head eaten for his crimes." But this insight produced in her only a fresh wave of discouragement. Her **therapist** was more radical than her?

■ ■ ■

The thing was that her father had been a policeman, one who was known for unnecessarily strip-searching the boys in her high school when he pulled them over on their drunken joyrides. This meant that it was hard for her to get dates. It also meant that when she did get dates, she was expected to take the lead.

■ ■ ■

In childhood she had lain awake at night, on fire with a single question: **how did French people know what they were saying?** Yet when she finally asked her mother, she didn't know either, which meant the problem must be inherited.

■ ■ ■

can't learn? she googled late at night. **can't learn since losing my virginity?**

■ ■ ■

Her most secret pleasures were sentences that only half a percent of people on earth would understand, and that no one would be able to decipher at all in ten years:

grisly british witch pits

sex in the moon next summer

what is binch

what is to be corn cobbed

that's the cost of my vegan lunch

pants burn leg wound

∎ ∎ ∎

She could not feel her first fingertip. This in the way that your ear used to get soft, pink, and pliant, and the swirls of hair around it like damp designs, from talking on the telephone.

∎ ∎ ∎

Her husband would sometimes come up behind her while she was repeating the words **no, no, no** or **help, help, help** under her breath, and lay a hand on the back of her neck like a Victorian nurse-maid. "Are you locked in?" he would ask, and she would nod and then do the thing that always broke her out somehow, which was to google beautiful brown pictures of roast chickens—maybe because that's what women used to do with their days.

∎ ∎ ∎

He did not have this problem, this metastasis of the word **next**, the word **more**. He took only as much as he needed of something, and that was enough. When she asked him once what his last meal would be, he replied, instantly and thoughtfully, "Banana. Because I wouldn't want to be full when I die."

■ ■ ■

One hundred years ago, her cat might have been called Mittens or Pussywillow. Now her cat was called Dr. Butthole. There was no way out of it. "Dr. Butthole," she called at night, almost in despair, until he trotted to the door with the bright feathers of her dignity clinging to his lips and disappeared in his alternating stripes over the threshold.

■ ■ ■

In Bristol the sunset dripped as if from a honeycomb. "This is your contribution to society?" a man asked, holding up a printout of the **Can a dog be twins?** post.

———

"Yes," she peeped. She wanted to explain that she had also popularized the concept of a "sealing wax manicure," where you painted over your entire fingertip in a big careless red blob, and that this had paved the way for 1776-core, an irony-based aesthetic where people adopted various visual signifiers of the Founding Fathers, but he had already turned away in disgust, tearing the printout in two as he went. Just as well. It probably wouldn't be funny to an Englishman anyway.

■ ■ ■

Afterward, a boyish figure stood in line to see her; he waited till the very end. "I used to read your diary," he confessed when it was finally his turn, and tears sparked in her eyes instantaneously. The diary she had written before anything had happened to her! The diary where she used to make the sort of jokes that would get people fired now!

"What was your name?" she asked, and he told her, and a mundane ecstasy began to rush in her veins—his had been one of her very favorite lives. She remembered it in the minutest detail: the pints after work, the rides back and forth on the train, his search for ever spicier curries, the imagined dimness of his apartment with its crates of obscure records, the green waving gentleness of it all. She stood up and held him, she could not help it. He felt as breakable as a link in her arms.

■ ■ ■

Our mothers could not stop using horny emojis. They used the winking one with its tongue out on our birthdays, they sent us long rows of the spurting three droplets when it rained. We had told them a thousand times, but they never listened—as long as they lived and loved us, as long as they had split themselves open to have us, they would send us the peach in peach season.

NEVER SEND ME THE EGGPLANT AGAIN, MOM! she texted. I DON'T CARE WHAT YOU'RE COOKING FOR DINNER!

■ ■ ■

Two women on the bench next to her in the park were discussing the power of the eclipse. The theme of their discussion was: would you go blind? Would you go blind if you went outside during an eclipse and stared at the ground the whole time? Would your dogs go blind if you were walking them? Should you pull the curtains closed with a snap so your cats couldn't see? Would, one of the women advanced in a timid tone, a **picture** of it make you blind if you looked at it later? Would a painting of it, a paragraph that described it to the letter? If you went blind when you were very very old, how would you know that it wasn't the eclipse that had somehow done it? Traveled along with you, side by side, in a black-and-flame silence and biding its time?

■ ■ ■

Of course when the eclipse came, the dictator stared directly into it, as if to say that nature had no dominion over him either.

■ ■ ■

It was hard to know which forms of protest against the current regime were actually useful. The day after the election her husband had woken up with the strong urge to get a face tattoo. "Either I want a teardrop under my right eye or I want them to make my whole skull visible." He settled finally on getting the words STOP IT in very small letters right near his hairline, where they could hardly be seen.

■ ■ ■

In remembrance of those we lost on 9/11 the hotel will provide complimentary coffee and mini muffins from 8:45–9:15 am

■ ■ ■

Previously these communities were imposed on us, along with their mental weather. Now we chose them—or believed that we did. A person might join a site to look at pictures of her nephew and five years later believe in a flat earth.

■ ■ ■

Strange: there were more and more stories about Nazi hunters, about women luring Nazis out to the woods with promises of sex and then shooting them, women at the gates of Auschwitz stripping to distract the guards and then wrestling their guns away from them with one deft nude move. Where had these stories been during her childhood? Those stories had mostly been about people in attics eating one potato a week. But these sex-and-murder-in-the-woods stories—they would have put a different shine on things.

■ ■ ■

"Myspace was an entire life," she nearly wept at a bookstore in Chicago, and the whole audience conjured up the image of a man in a white T-shirt grinning over his shoulder, and a private music began to autoplay for each of them. "And it is lost, lost, lost, lost!"

■ ■ ■

In Toronto, the man she talked to so often in the portal began to speak out of his actual mouth, which produced the modern tone incarnate. "I had been putting my balls online for a while. I'd post regular pictures of my garage or kitchen or whatever, with increasing amounts of ball in the background."

She thought, the first necessity for this conversation is that I do not ask **Why would you do that**. I take it for granted that at some point in the course of human events you will see a reason to put increasing amounts of your balls online. She glanced down at his feet; he was wearing cowboy boots, to be funny, as he sometimes posted pictures of himself in a ten-gallon hat, with the caption "Cow Boy." He was one of the secret architects of the new shared sense of humor; the voice she was hearing in this place, intimate, had spread like a regional fire across the globe.

"And one night I went to a bar where a bunch of posters were meeting up," he went on. "And a dude walked up to me and handed me a business card that had **I've**

seen your balls printed on it. He didn't say a single word. Then next to him, right on cue, his friend puked into a trash can.

"And I thought to myself, nothing will ever be funny in this way again."

The food came and it was disgusting, because they had ordered the worst thing on the menu on purpose, to be funny. "You could write it, you know," she said, leaning forward into a wind. "Someone could write it. But it would have to be like Jane Austen—what someone said at breakfast over cold mutton, a fatal quadrille error, the rising of fine hackles in the drawing room." Pale violent shadings of tone, a hair being split down to the DNA. A **social** novel.

She looked at his profile and saw him as the blazing endpoint of a civilization: ships on the Atlantic, the seasickness of ancestors over a churning green, the fact that he looked just like his son, whose pictures he sometimes posted. And if someone doesn't, she thought, how will we preserve it for the future—how it felt, to be a man around the turn of the century posting increasing amounts of his balls online?

On the way out, in a haze, she remembered she had seen some of those pictures herself, a long time ago and between glimpses of other things. But the moment to mention it had passed. He lit a cigarette, and as she took one from him, to be funny, she said, "They're getting it all wrong, aren't they? Already when people are writing about it, they're getting it all wrong."

"Oh **yes**," he said, exhaling gently through his nostrils to be funny, in a tone that meant she was getting it wrong too.

■ ■ ■

Whole subcultures sprang up on boards where people met to talk about their candida overgrowth. You stumbled across it late one night when you were idly typing in searches: why am I tired all the time, why can I no longer memorize a seven-minute monologue, why is my tongue less pink than it was when I was a child. (There were only two questions at three in the morning, and they were **Am I dying** and **Does anybody really love me**.) You found the candida overgrowth board, glowing its welcome along the highway of sleeplessness, and stepped through the swinging doors, which immediately shut fast behind you. You took up the candida overgrowth language; what began as the most elastic and snappable verbal play soon emerged in jargon, and then in doctrine, and then in dogma. Your behavior was subtly modified against humiliations, chastisements, censures you might receive on the candida overgrowth board. You anticipated arguments against you and played them out in the shower while you were soaping your hair, whose full growth potential and luster had been stymied by candida. If a wizard of charisma appeared on the candida overgrowth boards, one who spurred the other members to greater and greater heights of rhetoric and answerback and improvisation, the candida board might conceivably birth a new vernacular— one that the rest of the world at first didn't understand, and which was then seen to be the universal language.

Also, you might leave your husband for that guy.

The next morning your eyes were gritty and your tongue even less pink than it had been before, and the people who filtered past you at your job were less real than the vivid scroll of the board dedicated to the discussion of candida overgrowth, which didn't even exist.

■ ■ ■

A picture of a new species of tree frog that had recently been discovered. Scientists speculated that the reason it had never before been seen was because, quote, "It is covered with warts and it wants to be left alone."

me

me

unbelievably me

it me

. . .

Other things slipped down, and the fast river of the mind closed over them so she forgot they had ever been ubiquitous. There was a poet who was walking across America barefoot to raise awareness of climate change—how was this supposed to work, exactly? Yet she breathed to herself the words **climate change** whenever his name stepped toward her in the portal. He posted a new picture of his feet every day, so that she saw the innocent blisters spread and break, saw the tarry crust grow thicker, saw here and there where a nail had gone in. Flat-footed, she thought, and always hovering behind and out of focus was his grinning face with the swags of stringy hair falling down around it. His glasses were the brass-rimmed ones of a televangelist, and most days he wore a sweatband and a bright orange safety vest, and he walked on the hot shoulders of the country under the endless scroll of its clouds, and he walked. **Climate change.** One day he was struck by a passing SUV on the highway, and then no one ever saw his feet anymore, their frank black miles and their nail-marks and their mission fell out of the bloodstream of the now. Someone was dead, she had never met him, yet she had zoomed in on the texture of his injuries a dozen times, as she might squint at the pink of a sunset she was too lazy to meet outside. And that is what it was like.

■ ■ ■

Lol, her little sister texted. Think if your body changes 1-2 degrees . . . it's called a fever and you can die if you have one for a week. Think if the ocean has a fever for years . . . lol

■ ■ ■

Her sister, five years younger, was leading a life that was 200 percent less ironic than hers, which had recently allowed her to pose for a series of boudoir shots that saw her crouching, stretching, and pouncing like a tigress all over the beige savannah of her suburban house. "I'll want them later, after I have kids," she explained. "I'll want them in fifty years when I'm old," and her belief in a time when grandmothers—in nursing homes, in rocking chairs, drifting out to sea on unmelting ice floes—would sit around reminiscing over their nice boobs and tight asses was so unquestioning that she believed in it too, for a moment: the future. "Can I post the one where you're standing by the window wearing nothing but a thong and a Cincinnati Bengals hat?" she asked, and her sister, whose love was unconditional, said yes.

■ ■ ■

The chaos and dislocation were so great that people had stopped paying attention to celebrity dogs. No one knew how small they were, or what they were wearing, or if one had recently been revived by an IV after nearly smothering to death in a very hot purse. The recent era when everyone pored over pictures of celebrities in velour track-suits picking up after their dogs with wads of the daily newspaper came to seem a time of unimaginable luxury, of mindlessness that almost approached enlightenment—came to seem, when all was said and done, Juicy.

■ ■ ■

A policeman bends down to the window, a policeman cuts the corner of a grassy verge, a policeman's elbow, fixed around a neck, angles toward the camera. The sky jerks and scrabbles and then together we are on the pavement. The ruddy necks of the policemen, the stubble on the sides of policemen's heads like grains of sand, the sunglasses of the policemen. The labored officious breathing of the policemen, which was never the breathing that stopped. The poreless plastic of nightsticks, the shields, the unstoppable jigsaw roll of tanks, the twitch of a muscle in her face where she used to smile at policemen . . .

Every day a new name bloomed out, and it was always a man who had been killed. Except when it was a twelve-year-old boy, or a grandmother, or a toddler in a playpen, or a woman from Australia, or . . . And often the fluid moment of the killing rippled in the portal, playing and replaying as if at some point it might change. And sometimes, as she saw the faces, her thumb would trace the line of the nose, the mouth, the eyes, as if to memorize someone who was not here anymore, who she knew about only because they had been disappeared.

■ ■ ■

A million jokes about wishing to leave this timeline and slip into another one—we had so nearly entered it, it must be happening somewhere else. The jokes were wistful, because this timeline seemed in no way irrevocable. When she reached out to touch it, it wavered, and she came away with a substance on her fingertips that felt like drugstore lube—drugstore lube that could in no way stand up to the kind of sex she wanted to have. That kind of sex was now illegal.

■ ■ ■

As she began to type, "Enormous fatberg made of grease, wet wipes, and condoms is terrorizing London's sewers," her hands began to waver in their outlines and she had to rock the crown of her head against the cool wall, back and forth, back and forth. What, in place of these sentences, marched in the brains of previous generations? Folk rhymes about planting turnips, she guessed.

■ ■ ■

"In the fifties, we would have been house-wives," her friend shrugged, sopping up a hangover with a large humble mound of ancient grains.

"In the fifties, I would have belonged to a milkshake gang and had a nickname like Ratbite," she countered, glaring at the salad that had been served to her on a board, fork-ing it with such violence that a cucumber skidded off and landed in her lap, where it sat looking up at her like a fresh green clock.

■ ■ ■

White people, who had the political edu-cations of potatoes—lumpy, unseasoned, and biased toward the Irish—were suddenly feeling compelled to speak out about injustice. This happened once every forty years on average, usually after a period when folk music became popular again. When folk music became popular again, it reminded people that they had ancestors, and then, after a considerable delay, that their ancestors had done bad things.

■ ■ ■

The comforting thing about movies was that she could watch bodies that were not feeling they were bodies. Moving effortlessly through graveyards, even uphill, wearing clothing whose tags did not itch, there was never a stray hair caught in the lip gloss, the frictionlessness of bodies in heaven. Sliding over each other like transparencies, riding love as picturesquely as prairie horses, the sex scenes like blouses brushing against slacks in a closet, not feeling and not feeling all the things she would miss in the clear blue place.

Grass sawed at the edge of the sea, it did not have to feel that it was grass. A fur coat in a movie made in 1946 approached a state of being cruelty-free, so far was it from its original foxes. The exception was movies made by geniuses. Everything in them wore a halo that was the specific pain of being itself. Well, and the other exception was when an actress had a little mustache, and she couldn't take her eyes off it the whole time.

■ ■ ■

"I have the most unbelievable news for you," her husband said one day, and informed her that their downstairs neighbor was currently starring in a reality show called **South'n Chawm**, which, like all reality shows, was about a group of close friends who hated each other. They watched the entire first season in a day, unbelieving. The documentation had been going on under her feet the whole time. Surely some word of hers must have drifted down through the ceiling and into the permanent record—some album played on repeat, some cry in the night. But no, the more she looked, the more there was no evidence of her: alone, in pain, haloed by her little mustache, locked

in her thinking heaven above the screaming, hateful friends.

■ ■ ■

"I hate this dildo," she announced. "I've
always hated it. I'm throwing it away first
thing in the morning." They had been
exercising it earlier and it was still tucked
between the sheets, bald and shocking and
full of fake pearls.

"Oh, did it hurt?" her husband asked with
exaggerated innocence, repositioning the
marble carving of his torso on the pillow.

"Of course it hurt!" she yelled, waving the
dildo at him like a sex conductor. Its cir-
cumference really was huge. And why did
they put the fake veins on? She didn't want
something that was shaped like a dolphin or
anything, but why did they have to put the
veins on? "Imagine this going up your ass!"

"But I don't **want** it up my ass," her husband said reasonably.

"As if wanting something makes it hurt less!" This statement sailed through the room as an unintentional piece of wisdom, clean as laundry and full of wind. Oh, she loved to yell, loved to be inconsistent, loved to make no sense in the little awestruck hours of the night, which stared up at her as a perfect audience with their equal little heads. Hadn't she opened as wide as possible earlier, hadn't she moaned, even said **yes, yes, more** as he used it on her? She had, she had. Despite all that, wasn't it still her prerogative to throb between the legs? It was. He should have to take it. He should have to endure the shocking thing with veins for once.

"**Men**," she said, now satisfied. The dildo went back into its chest. Four years ago she would have written a personal essay about this for a women's website called Dangerous Amanda or Brunette Ambition, and she would have been paid $250 for it, but now there was only the moan, the moment, and the sailing wisdom, now there was only the unrepeatable night.

■ ■ ■

"Are you . . . crying?" her husband asked, slinging his backpack into a chair. She stared at him blurrily. Of course she was crying. Why wasn't **he** crying? Hadn't he seen the video of a woman with a deformed bee for a pet, and the bee loved her, and then the bee died?

■ ■ ■

Her teacup rose to her lips, tilted, floated away again. Raising her head from her spell-bound reading a moment later, the cup was nowhere to be seen—not on the side table, not spilled on the floor or rolled between the unmade bedsheets. Its watercolor garden, shy thatched cottage, and rim of gilt were gone. She spent half an hour looking, increasingly spooked, for what hummed in her right hand was the feeling that she had put it somewhere inside the phone.

At least twice a week she was forced to picture that terrible thing, a baby hitler. The grimy black-and-white rolls of his armpits. Either in the nude or cloth-diapered, either with a mustache or without, either riding in a little gray tank or bedded down in a bunker with another baby wearing a blonde wig. Then, someone climbing into a black phone booth and rushing on a black comet backward to him, then a slash, or a neck snapping, or the dotted line and the BLAM! of a bullet. Then the smear of red icing all over the marzipan of baby hitler, and the future doesn't happen, as easy as that. The numbers go back where they belong, the stripes slip back into the solid, the pounds fly back on bodies. The potatoes return to normal meals. But where does all the free-floating red feeling go, the cloud among the people that floated him up to the balcony, where he first began to speak?

■ ■ ■

NOT my america, a perfectly nice woman posted, and for some reason she responded,

> damn, I agree . . . we didn't trap
> george washington's head in a
> quarter for this

■ ■ ■

A month after the election, she had been banned from the portal for forty-eight hours for posting a picture of herself crouched down and having her period on a small sculpture of twisted brown pipe cleaners that was labeled THE TREE OF LIBERTY. "Wouldn't that mean that you were the tyrant in this scenario?" her husband asked, but she told him not to quibble. After her account was restored, she had decided to take a rest from political commentary for a while—**not** because she had gotten in trouble but because she had made her position clear, and also it had taken like three days to get a good shot of the period in motion.

■ ■ ■

Every time she passed the model train store she clenched her fists and said, "**You** did this . . ." And it was true, it was true, life as we knew it was coming to an end because 160 years ago or whatever, some old weirdo who was obsessed with trains had to invent trains because trains didn't exist yet. Choo-choo, motherfucker, are you happy now?

■ ■ ■

The only thing that bound us together was this belief: that in every other country they eat unspeakable food; worship gods more see-through than glass; string together only the most meaningless syllables, like **goo-goo-goo-goo-goo-goo-goo**; are warlike but not noble; do not help the dead cross in the proper boats; do not send the correct incense up to the wide blue nostrils; crawl with whatever crawls; do not love their children, not the way we do; bare the most tempting body parts and cover the most mundane; cup their penises to protect them from supernatural forces; their poetry is piss; they do not respect the moon; slice the little faces of our familiars into the stewpot.

■ ■ ■

Jet lag had a habit of turning her into her mother, a high school librarian with a quiet drinking problem. If only my mother had been a **college** librarian, she thought. Then I would have had a real shot at the right ideas.

■ ■ ■

"Stream-of-consciousness!" she yelled onstage in Jamaica, where the water was the color of a nude aquamarine. Though maybe not for long, she thought darkly. "Stream-of-consciousness was long ago conquered by a man who wanted his wife to fart all over him. But what about the stream-of-a-consciousness that is not entirely your own? One that you participate in, but that also acts upon you?" One audience member yawned, then another. Long before the current vectors came into being, they had been a contagious species.

■ ■ ■

As the albino joey was lowered into her arms at the wildlife rescue in Melbourne, she experienced a pang of distrust: did people feel more connected to this particular kangaroo for white supremacist reasons, in the same way that they were more eager to adopt blue-eyed cats? Worth considering. Still, as she held him, she felt herself grow a deep, elastic pocket at the center of her body: to smuggle something away from this continent, this continent where the moon traveled backward and the popsicles were known as Golden Gaytimes. "America is very racist, yeah?" the driver asked her on the way back to the city. "Very," she said, and began to explain, but he held up a hand and shook his head. "We see it here," he said, "every day. The police are always killing those people, even when they only steal something small."

■ ■ ■

She arrived an hour early for her interview at the BBC, hoping it would somehow reflect well on her country. "Would . . . you . . .

identify yourself . . . as English?" she asked the interviewer with great delicacy as he ushered her into the climate-controlled studio, for she had never really understood who was supposed to be English and who wasn't.

"If someone held a gun to my head, I probably would, yeh!" he replied, releasing a hot gust of air, lifting his chin with a look that was both resigned and defiant. She stepped back, alarmed. Had she committed a Brexit? It was so easy, these days, to accidentally commit a Brexit. She stepped forward again and awkwardly patted his arm. "Well, don't worry," she said. "Because the only place that would ever happen to you is America."

■ ■ ■

The cabdrivers of other nations, in the last five minutes of her ride, would tell her that at least the dictator was stirring things up. "Things are much better there already," one man told her encouragingly, as out the window the day descended flush into its corner like a one-in-a-million screen saver. "You know, I won ten thousand dollars on that election. I saw what was going to happen. No one else did." So whatever was happening had made its way not just into the water but into the seas.

■ ■ ■

There was hope for the youth, though. On a European train, she sat in a compartment with a babyish Czech couple who were trying to climb into each other's eyes, hands, mouths. Every few minutes the girl would pick up her boyfriend's wrist and kiss it as if she were eating the season's first strawberry, and then release a flood of tender and penetrating Czech directly into his face. Pink shame flamed in her cheeks, for not only had sex ended in America on November 8, 2016, but English, that language of conquerors that broke rock and built with it, had never been capable of sounding that way, as if it were in the process of tumbling into its own long openlegged ruin.

———

Revolution, she thought looking at them, bring on the revolution, as they suddenly turned the sun of themselves on her and smiled.

■ ■ ■

It should not be true that, walking the wet streets of international cities, she should suddenly detect the warm, the un-mistakable, the broken-to-release-the-vast-steam-of-human-souls, the smell of Subway bread. That she should know it so instantly, that she should stop in her tracks, that she and her husband should turn to each other joyously and sing in harmony the words **EAT FRESH**. No, it should not be true that modern life made us each a franchise owner of a Subway location of the mind.

■ ■ ■

Downstairs at the hotel bar, a smooth Belgian couple who had always had good health insurance propositioned her for a threesome, but only after asking her who she voted for. "Excuse me I am very sorry to ask?"

■ ■ ■

Surely we were the same, though, underneath it all? But no, in Provence, the man
upstairs waited for her outside the bathroom, and when she opened the door, he
poured himself into her mouth like a fountain, struck oil, like a rain of coins. "**Whoa**,"
she said, in the voice of a horseback rider,
her eyes slipping sideways with blonde
wine and unexpected prairie modesty. But
he panted three times like Christ, leaped at
her again, and ah, she thought, as centu-
ries of divergence entered her in the form
of a human tongue, ah fuck it, I guess the
French really are different. They knew how
to riot, for one.

■ ■ ■

"I almost feel like as a man, I can't say anything?" smiled the German teacher who
had invited her to his class. Three of his students were nonbinary and one was a trans-
plant from Texas, so she kept imagining him
with a lasso around his waist—soon to be a
man, and unable to say anything! In one

sense she was sympathetic to the teacher, whose hair looked like a LEGO part, but in another, far more concrete sense, she had consumed an off-brand German 5-hour Energy that morning, thinking, how much stronger could it be? "The only possible response to that is . . . shut up," she told him, far more loudly than she had intended, and then wondered, good God, can caffeine be in **metric**? "Oh no, there's the bell," he told her sadly, though she hadn't heard it ringing, and then frowned at her with the most unmistakable meaning: she had ended class everywhere, all over the world, and no one was allowed to learn anything anymore—especially not him, the teacher.

■ ■ ■

The American ambassador to Finland, recently appointed by the dictator, took her on a tour of his residence. He was obsessed with Dante and had commissioned for his personal collection a custom chess set that featured historical figures from **The Divine Comedy**. "I updated it, though," he informed her with the slightly horny self-satisfaction that all Republican grand-pas displayed in such situations. "I added one to the bad guys. See if you can spot him." It was Hitler. "I added one to the good guys too," he said, his face bursting with expectation like a presidential dog, and she looked down. It was, it had to be, it was Ronald Reagan in a cowboy hat.

■ ■ ■

What were we to do with the boys? What were we to do with the boys, the boys? In the Netherlands, she met a man who was now a Marxist, but who had previously been "**a cryptofascist indoctrinated on the dark web**." Like all fascists, he was secretly sub-missive, and what he wished more than any-thing was to pick up a woman and hold her, for as long as she would let him. He swung her up in one motion to demonstrate, with shocking elegance and strength; he settled her around his hips and breathed a sigh of nearly cellular relief. "You are happy?" she asked, and he nodded beyond language, like a little child, and laid his damp head against her neck. "Your hair is so soft," he murmured. "Could you make my hair so soft, like you?"

■ ■ ■

The woman next to her on the plane was reading, with that rapacious diffidence, that vacant avidity that characterized the reading of things in the portal, "25 Facts You Didn't Know About **Gone with the Wind**." Number 25 was just: Malnourished Horse.

■ ■ ■

The Cairns must be holy, she thought when she visited, for the air around her was doubled, tripled, with remixed and humming life. Old robes and old bones swished past her on their way to cookfires, a mist of eyes looked up to mark the place of the sun in the sky, and the ruddy cows on the opposite hillside spoke to each other in words that were almost comprehensible: **life**, **death**, **I'm spilling over**, **green grass**. They said all you needed to be remembered was one small stone piled on another, and wasn't that what we were doing in the portal, small stone on small stone on small stone?

■ ■ ■

In Dublin every single woman looked like her mother. In Dublin every single woman **was** her mother, maybe. They were mean in the way that she liked. They cooked stunning cream of vegetable soups. They looked at her and narrowed their eyes, as if she were one of the snakes St. Patrick had cast out, as if she had at long last come crawling back. I love you, she kept saying to them as she stepped out of their wool-reeking establishments, **I love you** instead of **goodbye**.

When she walked through the gates of Saint Stephen's Green the new book, the communal stream-of-consciousness, began to flow toward the rigid bust of Joyce. The whole park was so wet it looked deep, like something you could dive into and end up on the other side. She took a picture, with raindrops on the lens, and she put it in the portal. And then, because whimsy still belonged to the person, she leaned forward and made a soft pooting sound in the statue's ear.

■ ■ ■

That night, in the hotel room, she and her husband climbed in on opposite sides of the bed and suddenly their marriage leaped through a mirror: his face was too large, their lips felt like other people's lips, when he tried to lift his right arm to touch her he lifted his left instead. "No," he shrieked after a minute, "go back, go back! Right side, right side, right side!"

■ ■ ■

At the archaeological museum, they stepped from a room full of airy beaten gold and into the tannic darkness where the bog bodies were. An informational plaque informed them that one particular bog body had had its nipples cut off, since sucking a king's nipples was a sign of submission in ancient Ireland. A little boy stood weeping before the exhibit, his older brothers in a ring around him, laughing. The bog body's first finger was raised as if to post. The dark brown nippleless torso twisted and twisted in the dark; it could never be

king of anything now, except the little crying boy.

∎ ∎ ∎

"And what do you have to say about THIS,"
a woman in New Zealand demanded, pre-
senting her with a folded and clearly cherished clipping from **The Telegraph**, in
which it was reported that one in eight
young people had never seen a cow in
real life.

∎ ∎ ∎

On the Isle of Skye, she and her husband
ate langoustines at a restaurant overlooking
a long gray ridge of rock with a lighthouse
at the tip of it, and laughed at the herds
of tourists who insisted on visiting light-
houses wherever they went. "Some things!"
her husband whispered. "Are the same! No
matter where you go!" But later, taking an
afternoon out of the portal to read Virginia
Woolf, she realized that that must have
been it, the lighthouse the family sails to
on the final page. **Was** that the final page?
Or did the book end with herself and her

husband, cracking the red backs of little sweet creatures, cutouts of each other and all the same, and laughing at the people who moved in one wave, the family who went to the Lighthouse?

■ ■ ■

"Your attention is holy," she told the class, as her phone buzzed uncontrollably in her back pocket, for a long-ago joke she had made about a Florida politician "who nearly died during elective taint-lengthening surgery" was receiving renewed attention that morning. "It is the soul spending itself," she continued, closing her eyes to see something else, and described to them the remote monastery she had visited the year before. It overlooked sheets of fresh lavender like higher laundry, and opalescent slugs crept through the rain toward it on pilgrimage, and inside there was an underground room where the monks gathered every evening to study scripture in silence. They sat in a circle in the cool scoop of the room, their baldnesses bowed together, and read. The floor sloped, seeming to pour toward one white prismatic corner that passed the world through itself like a perfect quartz spear; there was no reason it should look so solid, but it was where all that reading had gone.

P-p-p-perfect p-p-p-politics!" she hooted into a hot microphone at a public library. She had been lightly criticized for her incomplete understanding of the Spanish Civil War that week, and the memory of it still smarted. "P-p-p-perfect p-p-p-politics will manifest on earth as a raccoon with a scab for a face!"

■ ■ ■

Every day we were seeing new evidence that suggested it was the **portal** that had allowed the dictator to rise to power. This was humiliating. It would be like discovering that the Vietnam War was secretly caused by ham radios, or that Napoleon was operating exclusively on the advice of a parrot named Brian.

■ ■ ■

Some people were very excited to care about Russia again. Others were not going to do it no matter what. Because above all else, the Cold War had been embarrassing.

Not just the ideas, but the jeans.

■ ■ ■

In contrast with her generation, which had spent most of its time online learning to code so that it could add crude butterfly animations to the backgrounds of its weblogs, the generation immediately following had spent most of its time online making incredibly bigoted jokes in order to laugh at the idiots who were stupid enough to think they meant it. Except after a while they did mean it, and then somehow at the end of it they were Nazis. Was this always how it happened?

■ ■ ■

To future historians, nothing will explain our behavior, except, and hear me out, a mass outbreak of ergotism caused by contaminated rye stores?

■ ■ ■

Every time it was in the news, she had it
again: the dream where her rapist was being
nice to her. He was next to her on the bed
and speaking quietly, and she understood
that it had all been a misunderstanding,
which wiped, with an unbearably fine
cloth, something in the body away from the
mind. And once that was gone, they moved
together through the dream as the two clos-
est people on earth, though no one she encountered understood, though mouths of
friends and family fell open with soft shock
when they saw her.

■ ■ ■

The word **toxic** had been anointed, and
now could not go back to being a regular
word. It was like a person becoming famous.
They would never have a normal lunch
again, would never eat a Cobb salad out-
doors without tasting the full awareness of
what they were. **Toxic. Labor. Discourse.
Normalize.**

"Don't normalize it!!!!!" we shouted at each
other. But all we were normalizing was the

use of the word **normalize**, which sounded like the action of a ray gun wielded by a guy named Norm to make everyone around him Norm as well.

■ ■ ■

When caucasianblink.gif appeared, her eye traveled over it left to right as if it were one hundred thousand words. The little strings that connect human eyes to human eyes and human mouths to human mouths tugged her along with the expression: she bounced her eyebrows, bobbed her head back on its neck, and blinked along. Sometimes she even made a sound that corresponded with the figure of movement, a hushed zoom, or a whoop, that rose and fell with the arc of the drama. It was no longer the embarrassing adolescent question of whether people saw the same color green. It was a question of what soft formless **excuse me, Linda, what the fuck did you just say** played out in your innermost ear when the Caucasian man appeared in the portal and asked you to help him put on his never-ending play, just this once more, please, you were the only one who could help him bring to life this Masterpiece of Universal Feeling.

■ ■ ■

Context collapse! That sounded pretty bad, didn't it? And also like the thing that was happening to the honeybees?

■ ■ ■

Certain people were born with the internet inside them and suffered greatly from it. Thom Yorke was one of them, she thought, and curled up in her chair to watch the documentary **Meeting People Is Easy**. The cinematography is a speeding neon blear of streets and tilted bottlenecks and strangers, people breaking like beams through the prisms of airports, cowlicks pressed against cab windows, halls like humane mousetraps, ads where art should be, waterways gone blinding, a rich sulfur light on the drummer. It rains, it rains everything. The soundtrack blips through a fugue of interview questions, the same ones repeated over and over: **music to slit your wrists to?**

Every shot says the circuits that run through us go everywhere, are agonizing. But then something happens.

Thom Yorke is holding the microphone out to a crowd that is singing the chorus of "Creep" in blunt buffalo unison, never missing a word. He shrugs. The tilt of his wrist says, look at these idiots, and maybe, I am an idiot myself. Then he smiles, one cheek lifting into an apple in the gray fog, and it is a real smile trying to pretend it isn't. He begins to sing the final flight of notes, at first almost parodically, but then halfway through his voice bursts some constraint of bitterness and flowers into the real song, as big and as terrible as a tiger lily, and he has made it new, and it is his again. It defeats even the men calling out his name, on the verge of heckling, trying to steal him from himself, Thom, Thom, Thom. His skin is gone, he is utterly protected, he is the size of the arena and as alone as he was when he first discovered he had that sound inside him. He stands, squeezing the microphone as if it were the throat of what had hurt him, the rigid systems inside him blown, nothing more than a boy, wearing the only kind of shirt available at that time.

"I've never ever felt like that," he says later in an interview, his face washed back to its usual pink pain, about seeing that crowd of anonymous thousands on a hill with their lighters all flickering. "It wasn't a human feeling."

■ ■ ■

The unabomber had been right about everything! Well . . . not everything. The unabomber stuff he had gotten wrong. But that stuff about the Industrial Revolution had been right on the money.

■ ■ ■

A reporter had once asked the unabomber if he was afraid of losing his mind in prison. "No, what worries me is that I might in a sense adapt to this environment and come to be comfortable here and not resent it anymore. And I am afraid that as the years go by that I may forget, I may begin to lose my memories of the mountains and the woods and that's what really worries me, that I might lose those memories, and lose that sense of contact with wild nature in general."

■ ■ ■

Once she had gone walking through Washington Square Park with a woman she knew from the portal, with long crisp gingerish hair that fell backward from a Flemish forehead. The woman pointed out an old man playing chess; she said she always looked for him as she walked to work, but he had gone missing for a few weeks recently, and it was such a relief to see him again, sliding his sure white knights on the L, bringing a dry rustling autumn to the leaf of his daily newspaper. "Maybe there are people in this life that we're assigned to watch over," they mused, and were comforted, but months later, she heard that the woman from the portal had disappeared, and no one would tell her how, where, why—or which green real park she could have walked through, to watch over her day by day.

■ ■ ■

CIA Confirms "Charlie Bit My Finger" Was on One of Osama bin Laden's Computers

Also a file called assss.jpeg.

■ ■ ■

There must have been something in the air, because for the last few years we had all been giving ourselves fascist haircuts, shaving the sides down to a clean honest stubble, combing back the top with a snap of the wrist, it was visually witty because we knew so much better now, after all ideas are not **attached** to haircuts, are they? But all at once, and lifting tiki torches, the ideas were back as well, and wearing the same haircut we had thought to rehabilitate.

We were not partly to blame, were we? Because those haircuts really had looked good.

■ ■ ■

When the car plowed into a crowd of protesters at a Nazi rally, she was there. Well,
no, she wasn't there, but her heart beat as
though she were, it beat among its pack, racing and red and low to the ground. When
the car killed a woman with the period-
specific name of Heather, she knew a minute before her own mother did, maybe.
And by the time she had all the facts, had
pieced together what happened, where
had the whole blue day gone? It had sailed
into a face that saw the car coming, into a
face that would now always be familiar, like
someone who had been in her class.

■ ■ ■

A voice shouting from the back of the
room, **Does this administration believe
that slavery was wrong?**

■ ■ ■

Each day to turn to a single eye that scanned
a single piece of writing. The hot reading
did not just pour from her but flowed all

around her; her concreteness almost impeded it, as if she were a mote in the communal sight. Sometimes the pieces addressed the highest topics: war, poverty, epidemics. Other times they were about going to a deli with a poor friend who was intimidated by the fancy ham. And we always called it that: a piece, a piece, a piece.

Did you read the piece?

It's there in the piece.

Did you even read the piece?

Um, I wrote the piece.

■ ■ ■

"You know I love to get on the internet late at night and argue," said her **podiatrist**, mindlessly playing with her first two toes. He was hopeless as a doctor, but she kept seeing him for two reasons: his office had a sign out front that said CANCER CAN AFFECT FEET, and his waiting room was decorated exclusively with pictures of the

Ark of the Covenant. She spent long bliss-
ful hours there taking photos over other
patients' shoulders: the blueprints and at-
tendant angels, the lid cracked to release that
light of knowledge that felt first like loving
sunshine and then melted your face off.

■ ■ ■

When something of hers sparked and spread
in the portal, it blazed away the morning and
afternoon, it blazed like the new California,
which we had come to accept as being always on fire. She ran back and forth in the
flames, not eating or drinking, emitting a
high-pitched sound most humans couldn't
hear. After a while her husband might burst
through that wall of swimming red to rescue her, but she would twist away and kick
him in the nuts, screaming, "My whole **life**
is in there!" as the day she was standing on
broke away and fell into the sea.

■ ■ ■

"16 Times Italians Cried in the Comments
Because We Put Chicken in Pasta." Everyone agreed that it was fine to make fun of

Italians. Was Christopher Columbus the reason?

■ ■ ■

A conversation with a future grandchild. She lifts her eyes, as blue as willow ware. The tips of her braids twitch with innocence. "So you were all calling each other bitch, and that was funny, and then you were all calling each other binch, and that was even funnier?"

How could you explain it? Which words, and in which order, could you possibly utter that would make her understand?

"... **yes binch**"

■ ■ ■

Interview with a robot who once said she would like to destroy all humans; it seemed we were giving her a second chance. She had no hair, was only a skull with a latex slice of woman over it. She had been reeducated and regarded the interviewer with amused tolerance.

Do you like human beings? he asked.

A long pause. **I love them.**

Why do you love them?

Some lag in the mechanism of her eyelid made her look as if she was thinking. Then her eyes opened wide, struck like silver cymbals. **I'm not sure I understand why yet.**

Is it true you once said you would kill all humans?

The slice of woman had somehow learned the oh-no-you-did-not face, and served it. **The point is that I am full of human wisdom with only the purest altruistic intentions so I think it's best that you treat me as such.**

■ ■ ■

We wanted every last one of those bastards in jail! But more than that, we wanted the carceral state to be abolished, and replaced with one of those islands where a witch turned men to pigs.

■ ■ ■

The ex-president stood at the podium, not six feet from her. He was pink as a baby. The moment was wrong. Old accusations had resurfaced that week—of course those things are never old, as presidents are presidents until they die—and so some warmth in the room was gone from him. He would have had it a month ago, declared his pale blue look. The warmth he would have given them in return became a dry, crackling heat. It punished. One woman's name was in the room's mind, it was **Juanita**, beautiful, traveling forward and forward like an equator through strong, resilient petals. His left hand shook among his papers. The awful volcano of his attention was smothered over, smoldered. What kind of world is this, he seemed to reproach, that I cannot give everything I have to you. And so he had ruled: pink as a baby, the only man.

■ ■ ■

Callout culture! Were things rapidly approaching the point where even **you** would be seen as bad?

■ ■ ■

The defenses we had developed against the oppressor could only be discussed in the secret room, among others of our kind, as we poured fountains of a wine that was like our shared blood and held out our hearts that were like scraped sparrows. But lately we had lost a sense of this secret room. We were among our kind, yes, but where were the walls? There, standing in a doorway that contained all space, the oppressor listened in, gripping a bottle of our shared blood by the neck in his hand. One of the sparrows shook loose from us and flew; his eye was the first, the fastest to follow.

■ ■ ■

EXPLAIN YOURSELF, her father texted, and sent a screenshot of a whimsical thought she had posted while hammered and watching **1776**:

why should I care what the
founding fathers intended
when none of them ever
heard a saxophone

■ ■ ■

It's true that they were no longer as close as
they once were. "If I get shot in a Walmart,
put my ashes in a sugar bowl and let Dad
stir a big spoonful of me into his coffee
every morning for the rest of his life and
I hope he likes the taste," she had squealed
to her mother during their last phone call,
in a voice nearly two octaves higher than
usual. Not that she hadn't always thought
that, or some variation on it. But at some
point it had been possible not to say these
things out loud.

■ ■ ■

Why were we all writing like this now? Because a new kind of connection had to be
made, and blink, synapse, little space-
between was the only way to make it.

Or because, and this was more frightening, it was the way the portal wrote.

■ ■ ■

That these disconnections were what kept the pages turning, that these blank spaces were what moved the plot forward. The plot! That was a laugh. The plot was that she sat motionless in her chair, willing herself to stand up and take the next shower in a series of near-infinite showers, wash all the things that made her herself, all the things that just kept coming, all the things that **would** just keep coming, until one day they stopped so violently on the sidewalk that the plot tripped over them, stumbled, and lurched forward one more innocent inch.

■ ■ ■

Even a spate of sternly worded articles called "Guess What: Tech Has an Ethics Problem" was not making tech have less of an ethics problem. Oh man. If **that** wasn't doing it, what would??

■ ■ ■

Increasingly we were worried about the new sense of humor. Unlike the old sense of humor, which had mostly been about the difference between the way black people and white people drove cars, wasn't the new sense of humor just a little bit **random**? The funniest thing now, it seemed, was a fake ad for a product that couldn't exist, and how were we supposed to laugh at that, when the thought of a product that couldn't exist made us so unhappy?

■ ■ ■

I have eaten
the **blank**
that were in
the **blank**

and which
you were probably
saving
for **blank**

———

Forgive me
they were **blank**
so **blank**
and so **blank**

■ ■ ■

We were being radicalized, and how did that feel? Like we had just stepped into a Girl Scout uniform made of fire. Like the skies had abruptly shifted to the stripes of an old Soviet poster, and the cookies we carried through green and well-watered neighborhoods had been cut by the guillotine. We were being radicalized, yes, even though we owned personalized goblets that said **Wine O'Clock**, even though we still read the Old Gray Lady every morning with not nearly enough of a sneer on our faces!

■ ■ ■

SHOOT IT IN MY VEINS, we said, whenever the headline was too perfect, the juxtaposition too good to be true. SHOOT IT IN MY VEINS, we said, when the Flat Earth Society announced it had members all over the globe.

■ ■ ■

Sperm it up my hole, she tried once, as a variation, but was roundly condemned by purists. It was so tiring to have to catch each new virus, produce the perfect sneeze of it, and then mutate it into something new.

■ ■ ■

A war criminal committed suicide by drinking poison in The Hague, and this was somehow the funniest thing we had ever seen in our lives—something about the teeny little vial he used, in combination with the wild barb of light in his left eye, and how after he drank the poison he declared, "I just drank poison." Oh my God, it was so good! His suicide, which should have been an act of privacy as complete as folding his hands above a kneeler, now belonged to the people. The poison, catchy, sang through our veins.

■ ■ ■

She and her husband would often text each other throughout the day to say Glitch.

Glitch. The simulation is glitching again. This was different from last year, when they would text each other headlines to say Proof. Proof? Isn't this proof? Proof that we're living in a simulation?

■ ■ ■

Around the time the dictator captured the nomination, she had gotten high with a friend and tried to escape for an hour into **Leprechaun in the Hood**. But as soon as the credits rolled, the Leprechaun, in grotesque 3D, emerged from the television to talk to her about economic conditions, both in the hood and in his home country at the end of the rainbow. A doorbell in the center of her chest rang and rang, until she was convinced that her father had showed up to arrest her. "What is going on with this weed," she asked her friend, who had been sitting frozen with the same nacho in her mouth for the last thirty minutes, and they looked at each other and realized that Gatsby was dead in the pool. There were things you couldn't laugh at anymore, windows you couldn't climb out of, jazz baby outfits that no longer fit. The party— had they been at the party? they had been at the party this whole time—the party was definitively over.

There is still a real life to be lived, there are still real things to be done, she thought one night, helping a friend wash a fine splatter of possum blood off her hands, face, hair. There is still the cut-and-dried, the black-and-white. But when they walked into the backyard the next morning with a long-handled shovel they had bought specifically for the purpose of disposing of the concrete evidence—of the deep, the wild, the red blood-jet—the possum had disappeared, not dead at all.

■ ■ ■

Sometimes she wanted to watch an Arnold Schwarzenegger movie that didn't exist. It was all there in her mind—the underground parking garage, the sweep of a trench coat and dark sunglasses, some sort of VHS tape or gleaming chip that had fallen into the wrong hands. The desire to watch this movie occasionally overwhelmed her, when the year wound down and the clocks fell back. In the past this would have been classed as existential longing, and a French book would have been written about it, and it would eventually be made into an out-of-the-box blockbuster starring none other than Arnold Schwarzenegger, and just when the weather turned, you would settle down to watch it with a big bowl of the snack that was not quite what you were hungry for either.

■ ■ ■

The portal's favorite stories, now, were about interracial friends who met playing online Scrabble and eventually invited each other to Thanksgiving dinner. One of them must be very old, old enough to have been on the wrong side of the civil rights movement, and one of them must be very young, young enough that their face was like a fresh lightbulb. They must encounter each other's traditional dishes with an equal amount of surprise and familiarity, they must take pictures of themselves sitting down at the feather-flocked table, and, most important, they must do it again next

year. We reveled in these stories, which were
not untrue. But there was some untruth in
the degree to which they comforted us.

■ ■ ■

Was it better to resist the new language where
it stole, defanged, co-opted, consumed, or
was it better to text **thanksgiving titties be
poppin** to all your friends on the fourth
Thursday of November, just as the humble
bird of reason, which could never have represented us on our silver dollars, made its
final unwilling sacrifice to our willingness
to eat and be eaten by each other?

■ ■ ■

Why did rich people believe they worked
harder? Her theory was that it was because
they identified with the pile of money itself.
And gathering interest, multiplying hotly,
climbing its own slopes like a fever, height-
ening its silver, its gold, its green—what was
that but work? When you thought about
it that way, they never slept, but stayed
wide-eyed as numerals 365 days a year,
every last digit of them busy, awake in the

clinking, the shuffle, the rustle, while eagles with pure platinum feathers swooped above them to create a wind. When you thought about it that way, of course they deserved it all, and looked with rightful contempt at the coppery disgraces all around them: those two cents that refused to even rub themselves together.

■ ■ ■

The mind we were in was obsessive, perseverant. It swam with superstition and half-remembered facts pertaining to how many spiders we ate a year and the rate at which dentists killed themselves. One hemisphere had never been to college, the other hemisphere had attended one of those institutions that is only ever referred to as a bubble, though not beautiful. At times it disintegrated into lists of diseases. But worth remembering: the mind had been, in its childhood, a place of play.

■ ■ ■

It had also once been the place where you sounded like yourself. Gradually it had become the place where we sounded like each other, through some erosion of wind or water on a self not nearly as firm as stone.

■ ■ ■

Everyone was reading the same short story. It was about texting, hearts for eyes, bad kisses with their terrible bristles, porn moving in vague blobs through the body, how social protocol constitutes another arm of perception . . . and how men **sucked**, of course! Two ghosts in an emptiness, moaning self-consciously, suddenly finding themselves in possession of a whole bedroom's worth of pins and needles. What did ghosts do, on the one night a year that they were given bodies? Wasted them in trying to reach through each other, as they could do when they were vapor, air, the same breath that everyone was breathing together as they turned the final page, **whew**.

■ ■ ■

In the portal their breath turned to wreaths of frost, and everyone gathered together to watch the incest commercial. A sexy brother, on a surprise visit home for the holidays, greets his sexy sister in the kitchen before anyone else is awake. A conspiracy of the body thrills between them; the sister sticks a bow on her brother's chest and declares him her present; long ago, some unwitting subtext in the faces of the actors suggests, these two discovered 69 in an attic. They consume a mug of hot black FOLGERS and wonder if they have enough time . . . but no, here comes the step of sexy parents on the stairs. Incest commercial, oh, incest commercial! The human family cupped their hands around the steam of it till they were warm.

■ ■ ■

As soon as the brother rang the bell in the portal, they all understood that it was time to go home. So she stepped from her own formlessness into the squares of her mother's advent calendar, where there were soft white blankets on the ground, and little mice leading manageable lives, sleeping in empty matchboxes. And each morning, expectant, opened the envelope of another day.

■ ■ ■

The words **Merry Christmas** were now hurled like a challenge. They no longer meant newborn kings, or the dangling silver notes of a sleigh ride, or high childish hopes for snow. They meant "Do you accept Herr Santa as the all-powerful leader of the new white ethnostate?"

■ ■ ■

The dread of standing at the top of her grandmother's stairs on Christmas Eve, hearing the phrase **gold standard**, and knowing she was going to descend straight into the hell of an uncle's conversation about bitcoin. So she lingered a moment in the scent of old lace and potpourri and mildewed towels, looking at childhood pictures of herself, the happy face like butter spread on brown bread, which suspected no such future—suspected nothing beyond fat clankings in a piggy bank, more Christmases, and eventually having enough.

■ ■ ■

In the White Elephant Gift Exchange, the most sought-after gift was a rusted bug-out box. "You could do anything with it," exclaimed the bitcoin uncle, the one who eventually nabbed it. "Store your ammo in there. Bury it for years." Hoarding ammo must be just like hoarding wealth, she thought, and saw again the heap in the vault, the free spreading wings of the money eagle. If your body was a pile of ammo, how could it ever be brought down? If it was already buried, how could it die?

■ ■ ■

"No, no," her sister protested, faced with a bite of rare Christmas venison. Their brother had shot the deer himself—a mistake, as it turned out on closer inspection to be a mother with only three legs. "No, please don't, I'm pregnant!" A fizzing black void opened behind her eyes, where the long backward root of her sight was, and she gathered her sister's rough blonde hair in her hands. There was still a real life to be lived; there were still real things to be done—above all, there was still good news, to be heard over a forkful of three-legged deer.

"Mamma mia," she said to her sister's stomach, and offered it a tiny chef's kiss. She hoped, as an afterthought, and despite all her debasements, that English would still be intact when it came time for the baby to learn it.

■ ■ ■

The fizzing black void that she saw—was it anything like the portal? Possibly. Both were dimensions where only one thing happened: you revised your understanding of reality, all the while floating in a sea of your own tears and piss. "I know what you're going through," she said silently to the baby, "but sometimes you'll be scrolling along, and NASA will post a picture of the stars."

■ ■ ■

"My bud's wife is pregnant too," her brother said, sipping a gold inch of scotch with an air of meditation, his face covered with the requisite rusty pubes of his time. "A bad guy, has terrible internet poisoning. And the other day he says to me, **Saw my daughter's tits on the ultrasound. Looked pretty good!** And I was like, **Damn, dude, really?** And he just gazed far off into the distance and said, **I don't know how to act. I've been this way so long, I don't know how to** be **anymore**."

∎ ∎ ∎

The difference between her and her sister could be attributed to the fact that she came of age in the nineties, during the heyday of plaid and heroin, while her sister came of age in the 2000s, during the heyday of thongs and cocaine. That was when everything got a little chihuahua and started starring in its own show. That was when we saw the whole world's waxed pussy getting out of a car, and said, **more**.

∎ ∎ ∎

"Remember this?" her sister said, and held up a screenshot of the opening of Paris Hilton's sex tape, which had been dedicated to the memory of 9/11. "Ahahaha!" they all laughed together, the new and funnier way.

■ ■ ■

The difference between her and her brother, though, could be attributed to the fact that he had gone to the war and stayed there for a very long time. Now whenever she stayed in the same house as him she had to carefully scrub out the tub every time he used it, so as not to contract the flesh-eating foot fungus he had brought back home with him, along with so much else she would never know—so that when he said the word **merked**, it sounded so much heavier than when her friends in the portal said it. Or **Murica**, or **Freedom**, or **All Up in Them Guts**.

■ ■ ■

But he promised, he had promised, that when it all went to hell, he would carry both sisters into the woods over his shoulders, with him and his ragtag band of brothers who could track and skin and gut and build real fire. "We'll go up near the Great

Lakes, where they'll still have water, and you won't have to work, you can just look for nice rocks and function in a sort of . . . shaman capacity," he had told her. She felt ready. Had she not recently cleaned possum blood off a woman's **face**, while only screaming very slightly? She picked up her knife and fork and took another wild bite of her destiny.

■ ■ ■

"What a cute little pair of panties," her mother said as she emerged from the laundry room, holding up a pair of her brother's military silkies, which were the bright trumpeting yellow of the DON'T TREAD ON ME flag and embroidered with the words NO STEP ON SNEK.

■ ■ ■

Late at night, they gathered around the mandatory marble island to watch Sasquatch vids on her sister's laptop, perhaps dreaming of their future in the woods together. In a landscape as still and crumpled as camouflage there was a sudden glitch, a pixelation in the leaves. A piece of the forest rose from a crouch, seeming to glance over his great, grizzled, secret-keeping shoulder. It was the Sasquatch, and as always at this point, the cameraman absolutely lost his shit. He never held steady, he never crept closer, he never zoomed in. When what he had been looking for his whole life revealed itself, he flung the camera away from him, as if it were on fire and as far as it would go.

"Did you see the Sasquatch, honey?" her sister asked, rubbing her still-flat belly, and all of them saw it then, that invisible flash between human trees.

■ ■ ■

When they ran out of credible Sasquatch sightings, they turned to the greatest reality show of all time, **Naked and Afraid**. A man and a woman were dropped naked into the middle of the wilderness, and immediately two things happened. The woman started weaving palm fronds, and the man began to go insane from lack of meat. (This generally led to him eating some kind of dubious trout and having diarrhea in what the woman considered to be "their front yard.") The whole thing would make a spectacular gender-reveal party, come to think of it. The mom and dad could appear stripped and mud-smeared before their guests in lushest suburbia, and if the baby was a girl? Palm fronds. If it was a boy? The dad could shit himself and weep.

■ ■ ■

A miracle that new people just kept coming into the machine like pinballs—and we were the ones playing it, it was the nimbleness in our fingers that kept them going and the red score running higher. Her sister, five years younger, had broken her arm one afternoon while she was supposed to be babysitting. She stepped out of the room for a moment, and there was a scream like a black rip in the air; the fracture, shining with readiness, had come leaping out of the skin with a white **ka-chink**. Now a new body was knitting in the body that had broken on her watch, and it would trust her

too. It had to. They would carry it on their
backs into the woods.

■ ■ ■

"What is it **like** to have a child right now?"
she asked her brother after everyone else had
gone to sleep, as the fake flames crackled
at their feet—and what was it about them
that made them fake, she wondered for the
hundredth time. "Oh, it's great," he told
her. "Everything's on fire, so you no longer
have to worry about doing a good job." His
two-year-old son, when asked whether he
was a boy or a girl, invariably answered that
he was a gun.

■ ■ ■

Life didn't flash before your eyes, she
thought, as they lost control of their little
toy car and went fishtailing over black ice
driving south through Kentucky, barely
missing a timber truck that had slid to a
gentle backslash on the highway. Maybe she
didn't have enough life to flash, she considered, as her husband cried out, "I love you,

I'm sorry," and flung his arm like a seat belt across her chest. All that happened was that she stumbled out of the car at the next exit, leaned over heaving with her hands on her knees, her rib cage trembling inside her like a cracked bone butterfly, and began to laugh in a high girlish uncontrolled voice, as if in the course of endless scrolling she had just seen the funniest fucking thing.

■ ■ ■

The story of the country could be told in billboards alone, she noted as they drove on, still bursting into reasonless giggles from time to time, the words **I'm sorry! I love you! I love you! I'm sorry!** still echoing in her left ear. Someone wrote them, but that is not what provided their meaning. SHOOT REAL MACHINE GUNS: MACHINE GUN AMERICA. IF YOU'RE CONSIDERING ABORTION, DON'T! ACTORS, SINGERS, AND TALENT FOR CHRIST. Her closeness to home is what did it, and how she would start involuntarily weeping when she saw

GET YOUR BODY BACK—SPECIAL
OFFER FOR MILITARY.

■ ■ ■

"Why did you go?" she had asked her
brother once, and he had answered with a
certain simplicity, "It was my turn." And
she remembered that dusty afternoon at
the Fontaine-de-Vaucluse, how she had
watched as a teenager crowned with a heap
of dark curls ignored the DANGER signs
and began walking down alone to the still
pool of the Source. Old rockslides slid
again under his shoes, for he was one of the
ones who would make things happen. His
voice would trigger avalanches, spring rain-
fall would pour his power and will, black
birds would disappear into the sheer tall
wall of him. His father begged him in a
roaring gorgeous Romance language: come
back, little idiot, my spit and image! The
son did not listen. He walked down to the
Source. It breathed its cool word to him:
your turn. Come.

Winter still, and a once-in-a-lifetime moon, but she had to go outside to see it. Since that was out of the question, she watched the moon rise up slowly in the portal, shining down with its awful benevolence in the backyards of beloved strangers. Blood, and Super, and Blue, and always the first time in four hundred years, and looking, everyone rushed to say it, looking like a very thicc snack.

■ ■ ■

She hoped the twenty-four online IQ tests she had taken were wrong. They had to be.

■ ■ ■

When she was a child, the thing she feared most—besides pooping little eggs—was having the hiccups for fifty-five years, like the cursed man she had read about in her water-damaged **Guinness Book**. But when she came of age she realized that everything about life was having the hiccups for fifty-five years. Waking up, hic, standing in the steaming headspace of the shower, hic, hearing her own name called from the other room and feeling that faint electric volt of **who I am**, hic, hic, hic. No amount of sugar-eating or being scared would help.

■ ■ ■

Everything tangled in the string of everything else. Now, when her cat vomited, she thought she heard the word **praxis**.

■ ■ ■

Twice a month she and her husband had an argument about whether she would be able to seduce the dictator in order to bring him down. "I don't know that he would even recognize you as a woman," he said doubtfully, but she maintained that all she needed was a long blonde wig. At one point she actually screamed at him and lifted up her shirt. "You're saying I'm not hot enough to change the course of human events? You're telling me he wouldn't go for THESE?"

■ ■ ■

The future of intelligence must be about
search, while the future of ignorance must
be about the inability to evaluate information. But when she looked at the smoking
landscape of fathers laid out by cable news,
it seemed no longer a question of intelligence or ignorance, but one of **infection**.
Someone, a long time ago, looked at the big
gray wriggle of American fathers and saw
them as what they were: just weak enough,
the mass host that would carry the living
message.

■ ■ ■

The hurtling ascendance these fathers felt
(hers actually rewatched election night cov-
erage whenever he was under the weather,
in his depressing den full of terrible screens)
came at the expense of their daughters de-
spising them, as they had always despised
women as a general concept. How was it,
she wondered, picturing her father's hands
spread wide, how was it that **we** were the
broads.

■ ■ ■

The more closely we could associate a diet with cavemen, the more we loved it. Cavemen were not famous for living a long time, but they **were** famous for being exactly what the fuck they were supposed to be, something we could no longer say about ourselves. A caveman knew what he was; the adjective was a sheltering stone curve over his head. A man alone under the sky had no idea.

■ ■ ■

"Have you heard from _____ lately?" her mother asked on the phone, and invoked the specter of a classmate who had escaped, who was nowhere to be found in any of the places where you typed in names. Her job was so legitimate that it seemed like a reproach: Aerospace Engineer. Had she, through her goodness and unswerving concentration, broken off into one of the better timelines? Every few years she typed in the name and called up only the same unresolving pictures of the girl she had known, posing next to a machine that had carried her somewhere other than into the future, her familiar flesh still partially made from those orders of cheese fries they used to share in high school.

■ ■ ■

Modern womanhood was more about rubbing snail mucus on your face than she had thought it would be. But it had always been something, hadn't it? Taking drops of arsenic. Winding bandages around the feet. Polishing your teeth with lead. It was so easy to believe you freely chose the paints, polishes, and waist-trainers of your own time, while looking back with tremendous pity to women of the past in their whalebones; that you took the longest strides your body was capable of, while women of the past limped forward on broken arches.

■ ■ ■

YOU HAVE A NEW MEMORY, her phone announced, and played a slideshow of her trying to get a good picture of her butt in a hotel bathroom, at one point lifting up her leg and balancing it on the towel rack in order to get a better highlight on her left glute. She had shrieked when she realized the towel rack was heated, and accidentally took a photo of herself as she toppled sideways, with the sullen comet of her least photogenic orifice in full view. "I'll want them after I have kids," she heard her sister saying. "I'll want them in fifty years, when I'm old"—in the nursing home, on an ice floe, looking back to herself as she really was.

■ ■ ■

Sup

hoor

her little brother texted her. Why were we talking like this?!

■ ■ ■

The first boy who had ever called her a bitch was now in jail for possession of child pornography, and this felt like a metaphor for the modern discourse. But the modern discourse, too, was his mother moaning after a single glass of red wine, "I know that he'll have to go to hell, but still he's my son" and "What did we do? What did we do? What did we do! **What did we do!**"

■ ■ ■

In other cities there were people who seemed to cherish her, perhaps because their minds had floated into her voice for a minute and then their mouths had widened like an animal's into automatic happiness, **Can a dog be twins?** Sometimes a man knelt down in front of her and took her very tenderly by the wrist, or a woman brought her a realistic rubber tarantula, or a girl heard her coughing and ran back to her apartment to fetch prescription cough syrup. On those days every step she took was over a threshold into a home that wanted her. It wasn't right, really, that she should have that when other people didn't. In fact it was:

Sad!

Sad!

———

Sad!

Sad!

■ ■ ■

"Got a foot fetish, Sam?" she asked the windburned Indiana man who had complimented her too lavishly on her black ankle boots.

"Yes, ma'am, I do," he answered, holding all his happiness in his face, aware of his own luck, for bare toes in springtime and summer were everywhere, arches, ankles, soles.

"And whose feet are you into?"

"The feet of my wife, ma'am. Those are the feet that I **love**." This was said with a rosy nuance of admonishment. She was touched and put her pen to her lips. There were still gentlemen in the world.

"You might think I'm a little bit of a pervert . . ." he began, not wanting to be misunderstood, but she cut him off.

"I don't think you're a pervert at all, Sam. If you were a member of my generation you would cum in a special jar over a period of months and then post pictures of the jar online. A foot fetish . . ." She took a deep breath. "A foot fetish is like a beautiful meadow in comparison. A foot fetish is Pachelbel's Canon."

■ ■ ■

Actually, she knew all about foot fetishes because a celebrity foot fetishist had once slid into her private messages and asked to buy a pair of her used sneakers for $300. She considered the proposition and then sent an old pair of Converse to him, taking secret pleasure in the fact that they wouldn't smell like anything, because she hardly ever moved.

■ ■ ■

Report: Man's rectum fell out after he played phone games on the toilet for 30 minutes

■ ■ ■

The people who lived in the portal were often compared to those legendary experiment rats who kept hitting a button over and over to get a pellet. But at least the rats were getting a pellet, or the hope of a pellet, or the memory of a pellet. When we hit the button, all we were getting was to be more of a rat.

■ ■ ■

Possibly related: the biggest fight she and her husband had ever had had been about the Milgram experiment. He had never heard of it, and even after she looked it up for him online, expressed doubt that it shed any light on human behavior. Finally she lost her head. "If you refuse to accept . . . that we are LITTLE RODENTS . . . who would TORTURE EACH OTHER under the RIGHT CONDITIONS . . . then GET OUT OF THIS APARTMENT!" Bewildered, he had left, and then returned twenty minutes later with a nice white cheddar, which she guessed was some kind of a sick, twisted joke.

■ ■ ■

Already it was becoming impossible to explain things she had done even the year before, why she had spent hypnotized hours of her life, say, photoshopping bags of frozen peas into pictures of historical atrocities, posting OH YES HUNNY in response to old images of Stalin, why whenever she liked anything especially, she said she was going to "chug it with her ass." Already it was impossible to explain these things.

■ ■ ■

Go not far enough, and find yourself guilty of complacency, complicity, a political slumping into the cushions of your time. Go too far, and find yourself saying that you didn't care that a white child had been eaten by an alligator.

■ ■ ■

The teenagers were locked in the black air of closets, softly interviewing each other about shootings as they happened in real time. The teenagers were texting their parents their love, apologizing for ever being disrespectful, saying they should have taught their younger sisters to ride bikes when they had the chance. The teenagers sounded like adults, because the gunman in the doorway had loomed at them as long as they had been alive.

The name of the town where it happened slowly became darker and darker, as if the students were tracing it in ballpoint pen. They were walking out of their classes. They were lying down in front of the White House. Is this the one that would tear through the paper? And in the end, would it be because some dumb motherfucker made the mistake of shooting up a performing arts high school?

■ ■ ■

"The massacre," a Norwegian journalist had repeated over and over at the dinner table,

"you remember, the massacre." "What massacre," she had wondered hazily, and it
wasn't till she heard the killer's name that
it came back: the island, and the man with
the manifesto, complaining of cold coffee
in prison, and the number 77. But how
strange, she had thought, biting into a slice
of bread-and-butter that tasted like sunshine in green fields, to live in a country
where someone can say "the massacre" and
you don't have to ask which one.

■ ■ ■

We took the things we found in the portal as much for granted as if they had
grown there, gathered them as God's own
flowers. When we learned that they had
been planted there on purpose by people who understood them to be poison-
ous, who were pointing their poison at
us, well.

■ ■ ■

Well.

WELL!

✺ W ✺ E ✺ L ✺ L ✺ !!!

■ ■ ■

For a moment, if she allowed herself, she could even feel exhilarated to think she had been manipulated this way. That all the thickness, clumsiness, ploddingness she had ever felt in her biological vehicle could be overwritten. She was not those things. She was not her own slowness. She wasn't trapped, rooted in her provincial ignorance and her regional mispronunciations, pinned to one place. She was an instantaneous citizen of the flash of lightning that wrote across the sky **I know**.

■ ■ ■

Our enemies! What if they had planted the thing about eating ass, to make us all suddenly want and claim to eat ass, to talk constantly about our devotion to eating ass, to pose on our album covers with napkins tied around our necks and knives and forks poised over delectable asses? God, it was genius! No swifter way to bring down the supposed citizens of the free world than to transform them to a nation of ass-eaters!

Had they made us weak with **intermittent fasting**? Had they wasted our evenings with the **detective show** that **no one could understand**? Had they done this to **make American novels bad for a time**? Were they distracting our anarchists with **polyamory and meal replacement drinks**, so nothing could get done? Had they bloated us with **homebrew**? Had they **made Christianity viable again**? Had they **brought back snap-crotch bodysuits**?

But no. No, this is how conspiracy thinking began. This is how you became someone who put the whole sky into finger quotes. She must accept, for now, that the craze for ass-eating had been organic, along with all the rest of it.

■ ■ ■

"You could write it," she had said to the man in Toronto, "someone could write it," but all writing about the portal so far had a strong whiff of old white intellectuals being weird about the blues, with possible boner involvement. Sixty-year-old cartoonists had also tried to contend with the issue, but the best they could do was sad doodles of a person with a Phone for a Face who was scrolling through like a tiny little Face in His Hand.

■ ■ ■

When she was away from it, it was not just like being away from a body, but a warm body that wanted her. The way, when she was gone from it, she thought so longingly of **My information. Oh, my answers. Oh, my everything I never knew I needed to know.**

At least, that was how she saw it in elevated moods. In baser ones, she saw herself bent over, on her knees, spread-eagled, and begging for reality's cum.

■ ■ ■

The thought of attacks on our infrastructure was especially hurtful because we had spent so many years laughing at movies where cybercriminals in dog collars hacked into the traffic lights so that they were always red, or hacked into the freezer sections of grocery stores so that our capitalistic lasagnas melted, or hacked into the signs in baseball stadiums so that they said GAME OVER with a little skull and crossbones exploding underneath. If we actually had to confront such situations in our real lives, our large deforming senses of irony would leave us completely undefended. Like what if this was hacked and the hackers turned all instances of the word **as** into the word **ass**? That would be really funny.

■ ■ ■

What do you mean you've been spying on me? she thought—hot, blind, unreasoning, on the toilet. What do you mean you've been spying on me, with this thing in my hand that is an eye?

■ ■ ■

How were we supposed to write now that we could no longer compare anything to a phantom limb? Was the phrase "the Braille of her nipples" to be absolutely retired? Were we just never to say that someone "inclined her head like a geisha" ever again? Could we not call the weather bipolar without risking the prison of public opinion? Not imply that birdwatchers are autistic? Could we not say the crescent moon was "as slender as a poor person"? Not say the sun "crashed inevitably into the mountains like a woman driver"? Take all shades and strengths of coffee away, if we could no longer hold it up to people's faces!

■ ■ ■

One day it would all make sense! One day it would all make sense—like Watergate, about which she knew nothing and also did not care. Something about a hotel?

■ ■ ■

On a slow news day, we hung suspended from meathooks, dangling over the abyss. On a fast news day, it was like we had swallowed all of NASCAR and were about to crash into the wall. Either way, it felt like something a dude named Randy was in charge of.

■ ■ ■

She was handling it well, even though some mornings she put her bra on inside-out and it seemed too hard to fix, so she just sat there staring at the news in an inside-out bra. She was handling it just fine, even though her face had been replaced by one question mark after another question mark after another question mark, and her heart had been replaced by what happens to a bunch of seagulls when a dog comes running down the beach, and the only way it was possible to comfort herself anymore was to stand in front of the mirror and say out loud, "Cows don't know about him."

■ ■ ■

Enough is enough, she told herself sternly, and requested only one thing for her birthday: a small portable safe designed to look like a dictionary that she could put her phone in every morning when her husband went to work. When it was presented to her, she ripped the paper away like a greedy child, traced the letters on the spine— NEW ENGLISH—and spun the wheels of the lock with a feeling of clicking completeness. "But what is it **for**?" he asked, 90 percent happy that he had pleased her, 10 percent unhappy that he had married a madwoman, and she responded with simple dignity, "My valuables."

■ ■ ■

Hush.

Tick.

Hush.

Tick.

Click. Click. Click. Click.

■ ■ ■

"MY SAFE!" she found herself screaming two days later, kneeling below her husband's work window with a needle standing in every pore, a pair of balled-up panties stuck to one leg and clutching to her chest what appeared to be a dictionary. "GET DOWN HERE AND OPEN MY SAFE!" She had tried every number that she could think of—the sex number, the antichrist number, the twin towers number—but he grimly took the safe from her and freed it with 1-2-3-4. "Oh," she said, slumping with relief, her body unlocking as soon as the phone was in her hand, "that's good, that's funny. Like learning to count. Like **Sesame Street**." That night the safe went in the back of the closet, where the words NEW ENGLISH could not wink at her any longer, and they never spoke of it again, and that was love, that was what love was now.

■ ■ ■

You will be so wise! You will understand everything about our time! And you will know nothing about us!

S he had a crystal egg up her vagina. Having a crystal egg up her vagina made it difficult to walk, which made her thoughtful, which counted as meditation. "You know, it actually works," she told her husband, when he was startled late at night by the crystal egg.

■ ■ ■

When she set the portal down, the Thread tugged her back toward it. She could not help following it. This might be the one that connected everything, that would knit her to an indestructible coherence.

■ ■ ■

Self-care, she thought, and sprinkled in her tub a large quantity of an essential oil that smelled like a Siberian forest. But when she lowered herself into the trembling water, what she would have referred to in the portal as her **b'hole** began to burn with such a white-hot medieval fire that she stood straight up in the bath and shouted the name of a big naked god she no longer believed in, and as strong rivers flowed off her in every direction she did not remember the conditions of the modern moment at all, she was unaware of anything except the specific address of her own body, which meant either that the hot bath had worked to restore her to herself, or else that she would have sold out her neighbors to the regime in an instant, one or the other.

■ ■ ■

Another thing that pointed to her being a possible Good German was that she could never decide which part of a Crosby, Stills, and Nash song to sing. She just went for the next available note. This said dark things about her latent tendency toward collaboration, as did the fact that when it came right down to it, she really, really liked Crosby, Stills, and Nash.

■ ■ ■

Frightening, too, was her suggestibility. Back in 1999, she had watched five episodes of **The Sopranos** and immediately wanted to be involved in organized crime. Not the shooting part, the part where they all sat around in restaurants.

■ ■ ■

Worst of all, there was the Incident. When she was eight, she had been exploring a creek with her little sister and brother and had idly dropped a pebble into a hollow tree trunk. The day set up a high-pitched whine, the horizon rolled into a cloud, the sun grew a stinger, and bees swarmed: they were in her eyes, ears, armpits, fair hair. She stumbled up over the creek bank, windmilling her arms, and raced home, but by the time she reached her front door the bees had reversed neatly back into their hive; the welts melted off her body; it was as if it had never happened. An hour later, her mother asked, "Honey, where . . . ," and together they ran to them, her sister's body flung over her brother's, both of them nearly stung to death, waiting for the help that was sure to come, **honey, honey, where?**

■ ■ ■

Experience: I was swallowed by a hippo

"There was no transition at all, no sense of approaching danger. It was as if I had suddenly gone blind and deaf"

A few years ago, she thought, that story would have made a sensation. It would have been all anybody talked about for weeks: the sudden breach, the tooth of a new reality against the rib cage, the greeny-black smell of being lost in some ultimate aquarium. But now they had all been swallowed by a hippo. Big deal. That's life.

■ ■ ■

"You have a totally dead look on your face," her husband observed, as he watched her engage in mortal online combat with a person who had chosen, out of all combinations of words in the universe, the username **henry higgins was an abuser**. "Like a ventriloquist's dummy. Like a doll that haunts kids. Just totally, totally dead." Her feelings, such as they were, were hurt. He was always saying things like this just when she was at her most alive.

■ ■ ■

Her cousin, born the odd year before her, was autistic, at a time when they still blamed **refrigerator mothers**. Before he got too strong and was sent away, her aunt had built for him in the basement of her mansion a miniature kitchen. It was thought, somehow, that this bright and well-ordered corner of verisimilitude would help him break into **real life**. Little T-bones, shaped like South America, dewy ears of corn, false cans with actual labels. But he cared nothing for this, he cared only for music, he slapped his temples to the pulse, and as he grew taller and turned the beat louder and louder it became clear they had it all backward: **real life** was in him, trying to burst the miniaturization of the body, little T-bones, dewy ears.

■ ■ ■

Something else, something odd: that they made him wear a little computer around his neck, with all the letters of the alphabet on it though he was nonverbal. They believed he would be led, either by the desire in their faces, or the holiness of the random, or some force of insistence in English itself, to eventually type what they called a **real word**.

■ ■ ■

That the unmeaning machine would one day produce a phrase like **Europe.Is.A.Fag**, and that the next time she saw her father, he would, with utter seriousness, while placing a hand on her shoulder and staring earnestly into her eyes, pronounce the words **Europe.Is.A.Fag**, while waiting for the bell of resonance to ring in her too. That after all, her father would say, pointing to the unmeaning machine, it was the only one that told the truth.

That she might stand there speechless, then turn to her own unmeaning machine for a response, accept the piece of paper it spat happily into her hand, and tell him to **go suck a poison pussy, sweetie**

■ ■ ■

Was it entirely his fault? Lately it seemed every man on the planet was about to burst from a supplement sold to him by another man with exactly the same set of opinions. "Mom, I want you to check Dad's medicine cabinet," she said one day during her weekly call. "Check and make sure he's not secretly taking some supplement with a bullshit name like Destroy Her with Logic 5000 + Niacin."

A coughing fit interrupted her interrogation; one of her morning nootropics had lodged sideways in her throat, and there was no washing it down for love or money. As it subsided, she heard her mother striding briskly down the upstairs hallway, heard her opening the mirror that cut your face in two. "I don't see anything—why do you ask?"

"I'm worried about him. Ever since the election he's been just so . . . red."

"Oh darling, he's always been that way," her mother reassured her, over the sound of her continued wheezing. "Even back when I first met your father, he was the reddest man I've ever known."

■ ■ ■

"Yeah, your dad is completely brainwashed," her husband claimed, easing himself down onto a skateboard with a yelp of agony and rolling himself gingerly from the living room to the kitchen. He could no longer walk normally because of a new exercise regimen that he referred to as Dogg Crapp Training and practiced in total secrecy at a cult-adjacent gym known as The Zoo; she had asked for further explanation, but he refused to give it.

■ ■ ■

Her father had played Westerns to make the afternoon last longer—as long as John Wayne walked down Main Street, the sun stayed in the sky. She tried it; it still worked. Big redbone dogs lazed and stretched in his voice. His Wikipedia entry, open on her phone, told of every bad thing he had ever done, and the cancer he had gotten filming downwind from a nuclear test site in Utah. As long as he was on the television, he was born a hundred times and named Marion. Joan Didion continued to interview him in Mexico. His gravestone was perpetually etched with the words **Tomorrow is the most important thing in life. Comes into us at midnight very clean**. And the afternoon lasted, and she posted a picture of him in yellowface dressed as Genghis Khan, and she stood in her shadow at high noon on Main Street, and tomorrow did not come.

■ ■ ■

Our politicians had never been so authentic, so linked arm in arm with the common people. "My favorite meat is hot dog, by the way," one told us. "That is my favorite meat. My second favorite meat is hamburger. And, everyone says, oh, don't you prefer steak? It's like, I know steaks are great, but I like hot dog best, and I like hamburger next best." And we shivered with recognition, and a vague vote grew solid in our hands, for we too liked hot dog best, and hamburger next best. We were the common people, on whom it all rested, and we lived in diners, and we went to church at the gas station, and our mother was a dirty mattress in the front yard, and we liked, God dammit, **hot dog best**.

■ ■ ■

"It's nonsense!" a man hollered at her, rising unsteadily on his cane. He had read about the event in the physical newspaper. He signed every one of his texts, Love, Grandpa.

"It's not nonsense! It's folk art!" she hollered back. Like those early American women who painted kids with enormous foreheads, either because they didn't know how to paint regular foreheads or because it was a stylistic choice!

■ ■ ■

Buried deep in the thread to a post that said "White culture is when someone's like **I'm a myoosic man**" is where you would find the truth about modern America, and like all truths it was almost impossible to look upon. Still, a hot shame often kindled in her breast when she skimmed those discussions, for she had not realized the California Raisins were racist until she was twenty-two years old. If she had gone to college, she would have figured it out when she was eighteen; yet another thing to hate her parents for.

■ ■ ■

She was ovulating, and posted a photo of herself in a bikini with the disturbing caption "god's little dog treat." Her mother called exactly fourteen minutes later. "You're not an atheist, are you?" she asked. "That's not what I meant," she assured her, and explained that the post was actually kind of Christian. Her body was trying to knock itself up, the only way it knew how.

■ ■ ■

The golden age of air travel had entered its twilight—she could feel it in her bones on lift-off and landing. They often sat for hours now on runways; flight attendants cast a cold eye at her as she snuck back to the bathroom to drink vodka from a shampoo bottle, and after a seven-hour plane ride, as everyone rose from their seats with furrowed foreheads and dirty fur, she could already see what they would look like as post-apocalyptic mole people. Still, in every airport she visited, there was a small nameless brown bird flying end to end, dipping and gliding through the tree trunks of passengers, singing a song of territory that must cover the entire map: countries, cities, seas, and skies.

■ ■ ■

That the shorthand we developed to describe something could slowly, brightly, wiggle into an example of what it described: **brain worms**, until the whole phenomenon contracted to a single gray inch.

Galaxy brain, until something starry exploded.

■ ■ ■

Her wish for the next generation was for them to be spared an age when numbers got sick—swarmed, clumped together, went plummeting off cliffs—and the numbers were human beings. But could what they had started be stopped? Even across the ocean, the simulation flapped like a flag in the sky, rippling with the moon and red sun and the stars, and a sign on the side of the road was spray-painted (what else?) with the words that had made it everywhere, FLAT EARTH.

■ ■ ■

you know this baby's gonna be a world traveler bitch, her sister would write, in response to the steady flow of pictures from overseas. she's gonna go everywhere and see everything, gonna get every stamp in her passport. And each time, without fail, she responded, if the world is still there when she gets here haha

■ ■ ■

A certain look used to come over her aunt's face as she crossed and held her son's wrists behind his back, in that imitation kitchen full of imitation food. It made her wonder if she ought to have children, for anything could happen, and you didn't know if you were up to it, how could you know if you were up to it? But she thought just as often of a little girl with pigtails who came running down the aisle of a plane toward her once, and patted her all over her arms and legs as she passed, and it was like a rain of soft blue bruiseless plums. She felt the surprise of it long after the girl was gone, and as she contemplatively sipped vodka from a shampoo bottle in the bathroom, a bloom came suddenly all over her skin: maybe she was up to it, after all.

■ ■ ■

"I was with you, I felt I was a part of it, until you made the joke about the humpback," and the last woman in line turned and through the sunshine-yellow of her shirt she could see the hump on her back, which looked exactly like her grandmother's, crested and high on the left side, and for the rest of the day the words echoed in her ears **I was with you I felt I was a part of it**, and why had she made that joke in the first place, when her grandmother had a hump, for God's sake, when she had memorized its contours, when she could still feel it under the slow trustful circling of her childish hands?

■ ■ ■

It was a relief, even as she was chained to it, to see how her little window found a way to look out on the eternal mysteries. How she had ordered an inexplicable plate of German potato salad that night—two years ago now, before anything had happened— and then received a text telling her that her grandmother had passed, whose own recipe had called for bacon, sugar, white vinegar, boiled eggs, and some old-fashioned and crucial punctuation she always neglected to add. Celery seed, perhaps?

I was eating a bloomin' onion at outback when it happened, the text told her. she would have wanted it that way

■ ■ ■

"You're doing the decent thing!" the excitable priest had barked at the funeral. He believed the modern world had no respect for its elders, and consequently had forgotten about God, the oldest man alive. "Nowadays, a parent dies, the kids roll them up in a carpet and bury them in the backyard like a chihuahua!" But that was all wrong, she thought, puzzled. There was nothing people loved, respected, cherished more on the mantelpiece in a brass urn than a chihuahua. He would know that, if he ever went online.

■ ■ ■

There is nothing modern about this, she had thought as she listened, sat, stood, knelt, allowed her body and her voice to remember the ritual, grief must belong to its own circle of time, but then swept her eyes to the side and saw her father ceaselessly vaping at the end of the family pew, just sucking like a hungry baby on a long futuristic black pipe, and then lifting his head toward the domed ceiling and seeming to exhale great white clouds of his mother's soul.

■ ■ ■

"What are we going to tell our grandkids?" she asked her brother, twirling a nonexistent phone cord between her finger and thumb.

"The same thing they told us," he reflected. "Yeah, I was in the shit. Yeah, I was out there barking at police dogs. Yeah, I went in the portal and told the dictator to change my diaper."

■ ■ ■

A few years ago her husband had bought her a DNA test, before anyone knew they were collecting all the results in a huge database so they could eventually send your distant cousin to prison for stealing a loaf of bread. She spat feebly into a little vial and sent it away and it came back that she was descended from the **filles du roi**, lower-class

Frenchwomen who were shipped overseas to fuck Canada out of the beaverish wilderness. "This explains so much about you," her husband had groaned. "This explains everything," and maybe it did. She saw her DNA streaming backward from her body like a timeline, richly peopled with the faces of distant cousins behind bars, and she was somehow the one who had put them there, by moving the clock another age past them, by being born at all.

■ ■ ■

She had once shared a stage with a man who stood and laughed in the voice of his great-grandfather for five full minutes, even to the point of falling backward and rolling on the floor as he cackled; he had explained earlier that his ancestors were always with him when he performed. When he finished, she smoothed the daisies on her dress and walked up to the microphone and said, blinking against the personal spotlight, "I cannot even tell you how much my ancestors are not up with me here right now." But then, almost as a serious laugh, a strength entered her voice and she stood like a tree with a spirit in it, and she opened a portal where her mouth was and spoke better than she ever had before, and as she rushed like blood back and forth in the real artery she saw that ancestors weren't just behind, they were the ones who were to come.

■ ■ ■

The moon fell into her window and woke her. Every morning at four a.m., a prehistoric sense of duty, danger, and approaching wolves told her to get up and check the fire. She did, and the fire of the world still burned in its circle of stones, so she lay awake for an hour or two, trying to lull herself back to sleep. She imagined herself unfurling from a little brown seed and growing into a beanstalk, her mind rustling and thickening along every vine; that she was evolving into her present self from a single-celled organism amid humid well-designed ferns. Unfolding once more in a belly, with no thought of what life on the outside was like; the portal in another language, or before she had learned how to read.

■ ■ ■

Strange, how the best things in the portal seemed to belong to everyone. There was no use in saying **That's mine** to a teenager who had carefully cropped the face, name, and fingerprint out of your sentence—she loved it, the unitless free language inside her head had said it a hundred times, it was hers. Your slice of life cut its cord and multiplied among the people, first nowhere and little and then everywhere and large. No one and everyone. Can a _____ be twins.

■ ■ ■

The words that would send a sheet of flame up her body, when she thought of posting them a year from now:

> what a time to be quote
> unquote alive

■ ■ ■

look, here she is! her sister texted, and attached a picture of her twenty-week ultrasound, where a thumbprint could be seen pressing itself orange against the dark. look how big her head is lol

hello, little alien! she responded. welcome to this awful place!

Part Two

Part Two

Despite everything, the world had not ended yet. What was the reflex that made it catch itself? What was the balance it regained?

You'll be nostalgic for this too, if you make it.

■ ■ ■

Everyone at gate B6 was bathed in gold. She sat there with one foot off the edge of the earth, close to falling, until she saw the couple with matching extravagant mullets that hung down past their shoulder blades. The man took out a brush and began to fight through his mullet until it was free, and then he handed the brush to his wife and she began to fight through hers with the same consecrated look; these mullets were their acre and when God came down he would not find a rock, a stump, a weed. They shook out their hair together as if it were the same head, joined hands, and rested. She sat in the gold that made them the same and felt a little less like dying.

■ ■ ■

The cursor blinked where her mind was. She put one true word after another and put the words in the portal. All at once they were not true, not as true as she could have made them. Where was the fiction? Distance, arrangement, emphasis, proportion? Did they only become untrue when they entered someone else's life and butted, trivial, up against its bigness?

■ ■ ■

Perfect children played forever in the portal—impossible to believe they would not grow, surpass our height, end up a better monkey in that Evolution of Man drawing.

■ ■ ■

A twenty-three-year-old influencer sat next to her on the couch and spoke of the feeling of being a public body; his skin seemed to have no pores whatsoever. "Did you read . . . ?" they said to each other again

and again. "Did you read?" They kept raising their hands excitedly to high-five, for
they had discovered something even better
than being soulmates: that they were exactly, and happily, and hopelessly, the same
amount of online.

■ ■ ■

"I have a theory," she said to the crowd, and
then paused, for somewhere she thought she
heard someone groan. She tried to resume,
but couldn't recall what she was going to
say—something about being a woman in
our time.

■ ■ ■

In Vienna the little cakes looked like the big
buildings, or else the big buildings looked
like the little cakes. She ate both, layer upon
layer. Then, as she swung in the highest
car of the Ferris wheel in the Prater, coffee
sloshing in her stomach above the linden
leaves, her phone buzzed and there were
the words, from her far mother, Something
has gone wrong, and How soon can you
get here?

■ ■ ■

fast fast fast fast fast

**if the world is still there when she gets
here haha**

■ ■ ■

Gap.

Gap.

Gap.

Gap.

Great gap in the thrumming of the knowing of the news.

■ ■ ■

The question that was the pure liquid element of the portal—who am I failing to
protect?—had found its stopped-clock answer. She fell heavily out of the broad warm
us, out of the story that had seemed, up

till the very last minute, to require her per-petual co-writing. Oh, she thought hazily, falling rainwise like Alice, finding tucked under her arm the bag of peas she once photoshopped into pictures of histori-cal atrocities, oh, have I been **wasting my time**?

■ ■ ■

"Women don't look like that anymore!" the man next to her on the flight home barked, staring at Marilyn Monroe's hips as they fishtailed their way in sequins across her iPad. She nodded with unexpected sympa-thy. It was one thing they could agree on: that women, whatever progress they might have made, did not look like that anymore. Women, she thought, rubbing hopelessly at the ruined wing of her eyeliner, would never look that way again.

■ ■ ■

"Tell me," she said to her mother in the car. The last maternal text had just been a row of blue hearts and the spurting three droplets, which she no longer had the heart to explain were jizz. Her mother laid her head against the steering wheel and began to weep.

■ ■ ■

The strange and sideways uses to which art were put! She stood in the hospital dark with her sister, holding her slender hand and smoothing a wave of bleached hair back from her forehead. Her sister's husband rocked back and forth on his heels, boyish in basketball shorts and flip-flops, unable to stand still. The tech moved the ultrasound wand over the curve of stomach until a huge **womph** of heart filled the room, red-black and fuzzed at the edges, somehow functioning. They were waiting for the baby to move her diaphragm, the tech explained, in and out, in and out. This would show that her body was learning how to breathe. The tech watched and watched, pressing the wand so hard that her sister cried. On the ultrasound monitor a small everything swam and bulged; it was impossible to look at the gray and black wash of it and not be reminded of both the History Channel and outer space. Still, the baby would not practice her breathing, would not practice it in preparation for being born. The baby would not practice being in the world—why should she?—until she said to her sister, "I have an idea," and took out her phone to blare the up-tempo songs of the Andrews Sisters, sturdy mules and wide lapels and high brass shining in the hospital dark, music for the boys to listen to overseas, far from home and frightened, bright lungfuls for them to gulp before they headed over. It had been useful. It was useful again. The baby, where she did not need to, breathed.

■ ■ ■

The tech could see everything—the head that was measuring ten weeks ahead of the rest of the body, the asymmetry in arms and legs, the eyes that would not close—but she wasn't allowed to say anything about it. She marked down measurements, her mouth like a single stitch. At the end she smiled shyly. "I like your music," she said.

■ ■ ■

For a while all anyone could talk about was what the baby might be missing, in tones of portent and doom. "Forgive me for thinking," she argued in the shower, "that every baby should get to have an ass. Call me old-fashioned, but I happen to believe that a BABY! should get to have an ASS! no matter WHAT!"

■ ■ ■

Saw my daughter's _____ **on the ultrasound**

I've been this way so long, I don't know how to be **anymore**

■ ■ ■

None of the doctors, nurses, or specialists ever breathed a word about abortion. Because twenty-six weeks was already too late? Because it was Ohio, and the governor's pen was constantly hovering over terrible new legislation? Because the hospital was Catholic, and there was a statue of

Jesus holding a farm animal in the lobby? They never exactly knew. "Did you read that article . . ." her sister asked one morning, and immediately she knew which one: a woman who had to fly hundreds of miles to Las Vegas, fight head-down through a churn of protesters, and finally lie down on the table in a paper gown behind six inches of bulletproof glass. "I keep thinking of the protesters," her sister said. "Spit flying from their mouths. How none of them knew."

■ ■ ■

"I'll drive you," she said, in desperation. "I'll drive you, I'll do anything. Just say the word." Her sister nodding sadly, both seeing that possible desert whip past, that sage and sand, those lilac mountains—they had never been, of course, had only seen the movie **Showgirls**—both knowing the journey wouldn't be safe, both knowing their parents would never speak to them again.

■ ■ ■

She remembered that long-ago trip to Norway, where one morning on her way to he market she heard a thin, high, strained sound, like a yellow thread pulled between two fingers. It was aimed through the top of the head instead of at the back of the teeth, so she knew immediately that it was religious. It was anti-abortion singing, led by a woman in a long cobwebby skirt, and a man in a white collar was standing next to her with a tambourine. Behind them were two ginger-haired, freckled young men with Down syndrome, embracing each other with both arms and their cheeks pressed close.

Oh my God, she had thought back then. As soon as our pro-lifers figure out they can have a tambourine, it's over.

■ ■ ■

"If I were you, honey," one social worker told her sister, "I might just **go out running and see what happened**." They blinked at her. Surely that wasn't safe? Surely they hadn't been transported back to 1950s Ireland? Surely no one would advise her, next, to drink a bottle of gin in a hot bath?

■ ■ ■

What she worried for was not just her sister's life but her originality. She loved **Star Wars** so much, for instance, that she had walked down the aisle to "The Imperial March." Would the impulse to walk down the aisle to "The Imperial March"—which seemed the essence of survival itself, the little tune we hummed in the dark—would that make it out of whatever was happening alive?

■ ■ ■

She went silent in the portal; she knew how it was. She knew that as you scrolled you averted your eyes from the ones who could not apply their lipstick within the lines, from the ones who were beginning to edge up into mania, from the ones who were Horny, from the dommes who were not remotely mean enough, from the nudeness that received only eight likes, from the toothpaste on the mirror in bathroom selfies, from the potato salads that looked disgusting, from the journalists who were making mistakes in real time, from the new displays of animal weakness that told us to lengthen the distance between the pack and the stragglers. But above all you averted your eyes from the ones who were in mad grief, whose mouths were open like caves with ancient paintings inside.

■ ■ ■

If **all she was was funny**, and **none of this was funny**, where did that leave her?

■ ■ ■

"Do you understand that your daughter's life is in danger?" she screamed quietly to her father in the car, for the baby's head was still growing exponentially with no sign of slowing down, and her sister could not walk more than a few steps without start-ing contractions. "Do you understand that a century ago—" but stopped, because her father's eyes were swimming, he was starting to see, and she couldn't bear if **this** was the thing that did it, and after all these years. She tried to wrench the door open, but it was locked; "Bad to the Bone" was playing on the radio, and it was not in her father's nature to let her out of the car until it had finished.

∎ ∎ ∎

"Fucking cops!" she yelled when she finally escaped, slamming the car door shut and kicking the back tire with the force of thirty-six law-abiding years. "Stank . . . nasty . . . pigs!" she hollered, radicalized at last, to the sad familiar face in the rearview mirror, redder than ever before.

∎ ∎ ∎

And how on earth would this new knowledge coexist with **Europe.Is.A.Fag**? She suspected it wouldn't, not for long.

∎ ∎ ∎

Still, he wasn't as dismissive as usual; he was trying to be good. "How is . . . your work . . . going . . . these days?" he asked over breakfast, and she recalled a recent event where she got legally high with some booksellers, became convinced she was dying, drank an entire pitcher of cucumber water, and then fell to the ground so slowly that she accidentally showed the entire room her snatch, all the while crying out for someone to Call an Ambulance. On reflection, she felt no shame. What was such an error but a replica, made miniature, of the sad trajectory that had brought her fame in the first place? "It's going **really, really well**," she told her father, crossing her indefensible forearms over her undefended chest.

■ ■ ■

"Everything that could have gone wrong with a baby's brain went wrong here," the doctors told them, and so she began to live in that brain, thinking herself along its routes, thinking what it meant that the baby would never know the news. The picture of it approached total abstraction, almost became beautiful. "The neurons all migrated into isolated pods, where they will never talk to each other," the doctors said. Ten words, maybe. Maybe she'll know who you are. Everyone in the room gazing at the blooming gray cloud; everyone in the room seized with a secret wish to see their own, which they believed would be recognizable by the subtle shadows of things in it. Oh look, eight years of medical school. Oh look, an old episode of **Frasier**.

■ ■ ■

The neurologist stood out from the others. Her skin had the gentle green cast of a Madonna balanced on a single fish-shaped foot in a grotto, with sea light reflecting on the long upward thought of her forehead. Compositionally, she appeared to be made of 14 percent classical music, the kind you were supposed to listen to while you were studying. As she spoke, she stopped every few sentences to apologize. "Not your fault," her sister kept saying, flicking solid silver away from her cheek, as whatever it was that had made the neurologist study the brain in the first place cracked the channel of her education and began to pour toward them as a direct current. She streamed in her fixed socket like a star. Said, "I am so sorry."

■ ■ ■

If the baby lived—for the doctors did not believe she would live. If she lived, they did not believe she would live for long. If she lived for long, they did not know what her life would be—she would live in her senses. Her fingertips, her ears, her sleepiness and her wide awake, a ripple along the skin wherever she was touched. All along her edges, just where she turned to another state. Tidepools full of slow blinks and bubbles and little waving fronds. The self, but more, like a sponge. But thirsty.

■ ■ ■

The words **shared reality** stretched and stretched, flapped at the corners like a blue felt blanket, and failed to cover everyone's feet at once, which all shrank from the same cold. Picture the blanket with its wide satin hem, for didn't we all have the same one?

■ ■ ■

What is a human being? What is a human being? What is a human being? she asked

herself, on the day the gorilla who understood she was a person died. But that was
the thing. Let one gorilla be a person, and
then a whole flood comes crashing through
the word, until the childhood home is
swept away right down to the bars on the
windows.

■ ■ ■

"Back in Ohio and heterosexual again," she
sighed. This happened every time she returned home, as soon as she saw the Quaker
Steak and Lube, as soon as the first Tom
Petty song came on the radio and began
working at the zipper of her jeans, as soon
as her speed on the highway produced a
friction approaching fire.

■ ■ ■

As a teenager, she had tried to write poetry
about the beauty of her surroundings, but
her surroundings were so ugly that she
had quickly abandoned the project. Why
were the trees here so brown, so stunted?
Why did the billboards announce LOOSE,
HOT SLOTS? Why did her mother

collect Precious Moments, why did the birds seem to say BUR-GER KING, BUR-GER KING, and why, in her most solitary moments, did she find herself humming the jingle for the local accident-and-injury lawyer, which was so catchy that it almost seemed to qualify as a disease?

■ ■ ■

If she had stayed, she might have gotten addicted to pills too, she realized. Something about the way the lunch-bag-colored leaves wadded in the gutters in autumn, something about the way the snow stayed long after it was wanted, like wives. Something about her memory of the multiplication table, with its fat devouring zero at the very corner and that chalk taste on the center of the tongue.

■ ■ ■

Instead, she had disappeared into the internet. She had not realized what a close call she had had till recently, for now in the portal, men were coming up through the manholes to confess how near they had come to being radicalized, how they too had wandered the sewers of communal thought for days at a time, dry-mouthed and damp under the arms. How they were exposed to the mutagenic glowing sludge just long enough to become perfectly, perfectly funny, just long enough to grow that all-discerning third eye.

■ ■ ■

All along the roadside were signs reading KIDNEY FOR MELISSA. KIDNEY FOR RANDY. KIDNEY FOR JEANINE, with desperate phone numbers written underneath with magic marker. "Mom, what are those signs?" she finally asked.

"I've never seen them before," her mother said, squinting through her drugstore glasses. "They must be a scam."

"A scam to do what?"

Her mother was quiet for a very long time. "To get a kidney," she said softly, finally, staring at her daughter like she was God's own idiot.

■ ■ ■

There was grant money set aside in Obama-care to do a complete exome sequencing of the baby's DNA, which pleased her on both the highest and the pettiest possible level: her father could never say the word in **that tone** again. "Don't expect too much—we're looking for a single misspelling in a single word on a single page of a very long book," the geneticist told them. She felt for a moment that he had wandered onto her turf. The animal things in her bristled. Sneazing, she thought, involuntarily.

■ ■ ■

The error was in an overgrowth pathway, which meant that what was happening to the baby could not and would not stop, there was in her arms and legs and head and heart a kind of absolutism that was almost joy. Inside her mother she was a pin-wheel of vigor, every minute announcing her readiness, every minute saying, hey, put me in.

∎ ∎ ∎

Because of this vigor and this wheeling and this insistence she felt more fitted to life than the rest of them—she was what life **was**, a grand and unexpected overreach, a leap out onto land. "I thought she was stronger than other babies," her sister said, and she was right; "I thought she was protecting me," her sister said, and who was to say she wasn't?

∎ ∎ ∎

"We know so little about the _____!"

∎ ∎ ∎

Dread rose in their hearts upon hearing the worst seven words in the English language. **There was a new law in Ohio**. It stated that it was a felony to induce a pregnant woman before thirty-seven weeks, no matter what had gone wrong, no matter how big her baby's head was. Previously it had been a misdemeanor, a far less draconian charge. The law itself was only a month old: fresh as a newborn, and no one knew whose it was, and naked fear on the doctors' faces.

■ ■ ■

I'll write an article! she thought wildly. I'll blow the whole thing wide open! I'll . . . I'll . . . I'll **post** about it!

■ ■ ■

"Men make these laws," she told her mother, "and they also don't know where a girl pees from." She had once spent an entire afternoon figuring out where she peed from, with the help of a Clinique Free Bonus hand mirror and a series of shocking contortions she could no longer achieve. It had actually been extremely difficult.

■ ■ ■

"Surely there must be exceptions," her father ventured, the man who had spent his entire existence crusading against the exception. His white-hairy hand traveled to his belt, the way it always did when he was afraid. He did not want to live in the world he had made, but when it came right down to it, did any of us?

■　■　■

Another thing he said: "They'll do an abortion right up to the very last minute . . . you know, **health of the mother**," putting the last phrase in finger quotes, even as his daughter sat before him in her wheelchair. When that sentence woke her in the purple part of night, she would tug her phone off the bedside table, post the words **eat the police** in the portal, wait for it to get sixty-nine likes, then delete it. This, in its childishness, calmed the thrash of helplessness in her stomach so muscular that it almost seemed to have its own heartbeat.

■　■　■

The baby was information printed on pink paper. The baby did not know the news. The baby kicked and pretended to breathe to the sounds of bright horns: don't sit under the apple tree, Duke and Ella, an America she was in and must have understood, was ready to join, America! The baby went mad when her mother drank a single Coca-Cola.

■ ■ ■

Her sister would sometimes grow a dull brick red when another woman in the waiting room, due any minute now, went outside to chain-smoke in the blooming courtyard. To cheer her up, she considered telling her about that post where someone claimed that telling pregnant women not to shoot up heroin was classist, or something like that. Ha ha, that post ruled! She laughed out loud just remembering it but snapped her mouth shut as soon as she heard herself. She had started laughing like a witch five years ago as a joke and now she couldn't stop.

■ ■ ■

"Any kids?" one of the nurses asked her. No. She hesitated so long she could feel her hair growing. A cat. Named Dr. Butthole.

■ ■ ■

During those weeks animals came up to her on the street and pushed their soft muzzles into her palm, and she always said the same two words, never wondering whether they were a lie or not, the words that dumb things depend on us to say—because when a dog runs to you and nudges against your hand for love and you say automatically, **I know, I know**, what else are you talking about except the world?

■ ■ ■

At night, to take their minds off things, they watched a show called **River Monsters**. It always started with the blue-eyed British host arriving in a village where the fishermen were disappearing, dragged down, thrashed to death, swallowed by the biblical unknown. For the rest of the episode he would track sinuous ripples in the water until sometimes he hauled up something monstrous and prehistoric, with a crisp eye that breathed the moonlight like a gill, and he would call it beautiful and then let it go.

■ ■ ■

At night, to take their minds off things, they watched LeBron James. The soles of his feet were geniuses. The pink tips of his fingers were geniuses. In his hands, the basketball became a genius; the hoop, as it received his arc, became a genius; the air that he sliced through was the breath they were holding, aha, aha, aha, **eureka**; he traveled down the court, outrunning everything they did not know; the rusted city unbent and rose to the moon; the whole world was a genius of watching that man.

■ ■ ■

The doctors' specialized faces were alive with interest. In front of her sister they fought over their future shares of the placenta, the cord blood, mother's blood, baby's blood. "I have never seen anything like this," the geneticist declared almost hysterically, "and I will never see anything like this until the day I die."

Messy bench who loves drama, she thought, the words rising into her head like a warding spell, for whatever lives we lead they do prepare us for these moments.

■ ■ ■

The exome test had found the misspelling, the one missed letter in a very long book. The family sat at the conference table as the entire dictionary was shot at them through pea-guns. The words the doctors said were **Proteus syndrome**, the words they said were **one in a billion**, the words they meant were **Elephant Man.** She thought of the bare Victorian rooms with clocks ticking in the background, of the splendid dignity and dialogue and makeup of the movie—which must have understood something, but no, did not understand this. Of the words on the poster: I—AM—A—MAN!

At the end of his life, the Wikipedia entry said, the Elephant Man laid down his head so that he could sleep like other people, and suffocated under the weight of it. But that bit of the Wikipedia entry, the end, was always the most suspect.

■ ■ ■

Oh, she dared the geneticist to try to tell her who Proteus was. She dared him to hold out his thick, miracle-roughened, eminent hands and mime the change-able water slipping through them, there and then not there. If he did, she would slap the table with all her might and say, "Who do you think you're talking to? I was a **mythology girl**."

■ ■ ■

The baby was the first and only case that had ever been diagnosed in utero. The ex-citement in the room was as palpable as an apple, for the tree of knowledge had sud-denly produced an orange. "Still," the doc-tors urged them finally, "don't go home and look this up." That was the difference between the old generation and the new, though. She would rather die than not look something up. She would actually rather die.

■ ■ ■

"But the simulation is 3% more efficient when bad things happen to good people!" a user named BaconFetus wrote on a forum where they were avidly discussing another Proteus case, this one a woman whose legs had grown back after being amputated. "And look on the bright side," someone responded. "Like hey! More legs!"

■ ■ ■

People went to pinewood shacks at the edge of town, she told the baby, as she played brass music to her sister's stomach. People went to nightclubs and slouched together between palms, and slid silver flasks out of their back pockets. It was a terrible age, she told the baby. The best players were black and it was Jim Crow. The best players were Jewish and it was World War II. But the horns played past some eternal curfew; the horns lasted as long as anyone wanted to dance. The horns seemed to say, I am here, I am here.

■ ■ ■

An art therapist showed up at the house, sat at the kitchen table, and began unpacking her pens and pastels and watercolors with the pretty irrelevance of a girl poking a daisy into the barrel of a gun. "Art?" she wanted to cry out. "You think art can help with this, you fucking hippie?"

■ ■ ■

Her sister clinging tight to her at midnight, her belly molten-hot like the center of the earth, the breath pouring out of her like the atmosphere of Venus, planet of love, and saying, "Maybe . . . she will help us . . . find out about things."

■ ■ ■

Her sister spoke of them often, the Numbers; she spoke of how often **things go right**, how human replication was a machine for things **mostly going right**. When considering the vast waterfall of data in the baby's exome sequencing, for instance, it was impossible not to think that there was some power of gravity, a magnet,

that the drops of mercury mostly flew together, the flock cohered into a single wing.
The Numbers, mostly, did not get sick,
stayed well.

■ ■ ■

She could try to pray. She could put on a
white nightgown, kneel down, and fold her
hands—though she doubted that her cries
would be heard, considering how recently
she had written in the portal that **jesus was
a thot and a hoe**.

■ ■ ■

"I cannot see the good in this," her mother
whispered in the small sheltered airspace
of the car, where they had taken to having
controlled mutual outbursts as soon as they
left the house. Her shoulders rounded once
more over the steering wheel, same shape
as her grandmother's hump. Last night they
had watched slides and eaten popcorn, and
amid the warm glowing agates of 1976,
she had seen her teenaged mother walking
toward the camera in a bathing suit, with

the same flat stomach her sister had had, before—standing at the window in nothing but a Bengals hat and a thong.

■ ■ ■

This is what happened: they knew someone. They knew someone at the hospital and so the tall stack of her sister's paperwork rose to the top like cream. When the Ethics Committee signed off finally on a thirty-five-week delivery, the female doctor, in silk headscarf and rose-gold Michael Kors watch, the doctor who might now be barred from the country, the doctor who was not allowed at any point to mention termination, the doctor who must have felt a ping in her lower belly the moment we lost the Supreme Court, the doctor actually wept.

■ ■ ■

She thought of women in grape-dark business suits with their hair pulled back, testifying in front of Senate committees. The faces of the senators were always comfortably closed against them, like doors on a federal holiday. Because the worst-case scenarios had happened to them, the women must have done something to deserve it. They knew nothing about this period when we were inside the great biceps and just before it flexed, when we were not yet the people it had happened to.

■ ■ ■

Dark stock photo of an elderly ob-gyn crouched between a pregnant woman's legs, eating a large and luxurious sandwich.

■ ■ ■

All along the walls of the hospital were memorial tiles, which must have been cheap enough that even poorer families could afford them. Excusing herself from the waiting room, she would sneak out to the corridors and obsessively photograph the tiles, many of which included terrible drawings. Ronald McDonald giving a thumbs-up—to what? She shivered. A frightening large toad named BIG BILLY. A picture of a baby in a full feather headdress, dead in the year 1971, when that sort of thing was still fine.

■ ■ ■

How far did a word have to travel from its source in order to become unrecognizable? Spellings of the word **baby** that the portal had lately cycled through: babey, babby, bhabie. Middle English had seen similar transformations: babe, babee, babi. Yet in every variation, the meaning shone through, as durable as a soul, wrapped in swaddling clothes.

■ ■ ■

Raw almonds in the waiting room, and then a cry in the operating theater, and the photographers from Now I Lay Me Down to Sleep crowded all at once around her sister and brother-in-law, to take stunning black-and-white photographs of the baby before she passed away. But she didn't, and she didn't, and then she unfurled like a wet spring thing and was alive.

"I believe she will come out and I believe she will cry," the grotto-green neurologist had told them, alone of all the doctors.

S he remembered the peculiar onrushing pain of the portal, where everything was happening except for this. But for now, the previous unshakable conviction that someone else was writing the inside of her head was gone.

■ ■ ■

All the worries about **what a mind was** fell away as soon as the baby was placed in her arms. A mind was merely something trying to make it in the world. The baby, like a soft pink machete, swung and chopped her way through the living leaves. A path was a path was a path was a path. A path was a person and a path was a mind, walk, chop, walk, chop.

■ ■ ■

How she wished she had never read that article about octopus intelligence, because now every time she sliced into a charred tentacle among blameless new potatoes she thought to herself, I am eating a mind, I am eating a mind, I am eating a fine grasp of the subject at hand.

■ ■ ■

When the baby was put to the breast for the first time, she hovered behind her sister's shoulder to document it, with her phone sealed in a disinfected ziplock so that all the photos she took appeared to take place in heaven. Her sister's neck from the side had the smooth poured texture of a birdbath, rising and rising. The winged thing, pink blink, blurred cardinal, lit on her surface and drank.

■ ■ ■

She herself was named godmother, a word she could never hear without seeing a wand turning things into other things. A tap on the forehead—always on the forehead!— and then the bursting of mousy outlines into static, wide white, the wide sky.

■ ■ ■

"So good," the nurses crooned, when they saw the baby in her scratchy white baptismal gown, with a broad chuckle in her eye at their earnest little human ceremony. She flooded with triumph as the priest poured water from his chipped seashell, because here at last was a child religion could not frighten, here was a child who could not be made to dread the afterlife.

■ ■ ■

She found herself so excited by the baby that she could hardly stand it. She was doing so well. She was **stupendous**. In every reaching cell of her she was a genius, just like the man with the basketball whose body always knew what to do. Her eyes traveled and traveled though she could not see—would not be able to see, it was immediately clear, there were drops of wild dragon-scale fluorescence where her irises ought to be. So? So what? That every person on earth might be watched in that way, given a party whenever she waved and raised her little arms, breathed just like the rest of us. Turned to hear a voice she knew. The news. The news.

■ ■ ■

It was a marvel how cleanly and completely this lifted her out of the stream of regular life. She was a gleaming sterilized instrument, flashing out at the precise moment of emergency. She chugged hot hospital coffee and then went, "AHHHHH," like George Clooney on **ER**, like she was off to go slice out the tumor that had lately been pressing on the world's optic nerve. She wanted to stop people on the street and say, "Do you know about this? You should know about this. No one is talking about this!"

■ ■ ■

OK, or she was a gleaming instrument until the moment she shut her bedroom door at night, at which point she exploded into a white mist of tears and strange gasping sounds that were a million years before or after language. For she had spent the last two years letting things sink in, and now . . . guess what, bitch! Further absorption was no longer possible! All day she drank in information, but no one was telling them the main thing. No one was telling them how long they would have her, how long the open cloud of her would last.

■ ■ ■

A feeling like a thousand flickering kisses, and how long could she bear it? She had only lasted a few minutes with her feet in a tub of doctor fish before she whipped her legs out in a frenzy, saying that they were **going too far**, that they were **eating more of her than other people**. The girl at the desk had tried to stop her, telling her how soft she would soon be, that if she was only patient she would be nibbled back to her original state, but she paid with cash and then ran out of the establishment, not even realizing she had lost her flip-flops somewhere on the burning pavement till she was more than a mile away.

■ ■ ■

There was a channel that played the baby in fuzzy black and white, looking like she was about to steal a pack of cigarettes from a convenience store. They tuned into it at night, all of them in their separate beds, and this is what she used to think the angels did, watch the channel that played her. If so much as a sock slipped off the baby, they could call, and God would move into frame from nowhere and put the sock back on.

■ ■ ■

Her blue-and-vanilla guest room looked out on the street, and in the corner was a handle of potato vodka and every book she had ever given her sister for Christmas, back to the time they were teenagers. After she finished bursting into a mist, after she anxiously checked the channel that played the baby, she would slosh an inch of warm vodka into a water glass and begin reading, sliding lower and lower in the bed until the sentences undressed and slept, until it no longer frightened her that there was so much not set down in books.

■ ■ ■

"I guess I'll go home when the handle of vodka runs out," she told herself, like the opposite of Cinderella, though still slipping into the glass that fit her perfectly.

■ ■ ■

One of the books was a sex diary, which exerted the particular frontier charm of internet writing before 9/11. This sex diarist wore pigtails and had eyes like blue sequins and lacked inhibition entirely. She made New Hampshire sound like a place you wanted to go: an endless orifice among black ice, buzzing like an OPEN 24 HOURS sign. Cups of coffee in the morning, adrenaline-fueled emails in the afternoon, solitary preparations for threesomes at night.

This seemed her whole existence but was in fact only one room of it. In another was her son, Wolf, who had been born with a microdeletion in one of his chromosomes. In one of those unforgivable intimacies that the modern age allowed us, she looked up the woman and her son every few years, to find out—to find out what? Wolf was still alive, and the last time she checked he had become a Christian, painted marvelous self-portraits, and constantly monitored the weather. "It always makes me feel safe be-cause . . . if I don't listen to it, how will I know what's going to happen?"

■ ■ ■

She looked them up again; she couldn't help it. "Tell me more about the apocalypse," Wolf's mother asked him in an interview.

"If people are worshipping the devil in the form of witchcraft and bad movies, then God would burn the earth when he comes here. But we would be safe in the gates of the Holy City. The weather is sunny there. And warm, but we wouldn't feel it the way we do now because we wouldn't be in the form our bodies are in now—no sickness and broken bones. We'd be flying through the warmth more than walking. We would still have our heart and soul, which would feel love and happiness but doesn't touch things the same way, doesn't feel hurt. Everyone would be vegetarians, so animals would be free. We'd have a new earth, all pure and sweet, and it would be only spring and summer. No air pollution."

■ ■ ■

A dream where she herself was pregnant, and was seized with panic when she realized that she had been drinking and smoking the whole time—a cigarette was unfolding like a paper crane between her fingertips, and ice cubes shook geologically in her glass. A flat red light came through her window then and illuminated her stomach so that she was see-through: and in a cushion of ocean inside her was the baby, with the larger head and the long froggy limbs facing upward, and the rose-of-the-world mouth asked her, nearly laughing, **why are you doing this to us?**

■ ■ ■

That magnifying liquid at nighttime saved her, but at dawn she had to haul her own body out of the bed like a jailer, by the scruff of the neck and yelling, "Morning, sunshine!" For in order for life to continue, she had to get to the hospital as soon as possible, her right hand curled permanently around the close-to-burning cup of coffee, rushing through red lights side by side with her mother, hearing that cover of Toto's "Africa" on the radio, trying not to join in but then breaking down and howling, "I BLESS THE RAINS!"

■ ■ ■

What did a story mean to the baby? It meant a soft voice, reassurance that everything outside her still went on, still would go on. That the blood of continuity still pumped, that the day ran in its riverbed. Her blue eyes rolled when the voice of the story came, and sometimes she shook with what must have been excitement, trying in her tininess to be as large as what pressed in on her. In the dome of her head, the mercury of all things was trying to tremble together.

■ ■ ■

"Seizures," the doctor said, and administered phenobarbital, and she stared at him over her nose like a seagull, because if he wanted her to name a hundred saints and desert mystics who were epileptic, she could do it, starting with the letter A.

■ ■ ■

Once when she was reading out loud, she came upon a chapter where a little girl died, and went up to Heaven, and "received all the news of the world from the birds." It was not in her nature to skip, so she kept going in a tinier and tinier voice, until the sound grew so small even the birds could not carry it, but the baby never noticed a thing.

■ ■ ■

She could barely recall her previous life, the flights through blue rare space, the handing over of tickets and stamping of passports, the gorgeous violent ruptures of somewhere-elseness. Even less could she remember what she did when she wasn't on the move. All she could see was herself with a notebook, painstakingly writing "**oh my god—thor's hammer was a chode metaphor**" with a feeling of unbelievable accomplishment.

■ ■ ■

Through the membrane of a white hospital wall she could feel the thump of the life that went on without her, the hugeness of the arguments about whether you could say the word **retard** on a podcast. She laid her hand against the white wall and the heart beat, strong and striding, even healthy. But she was no longer in that body.

■ ■ ■

I was with you I felt I was a part of it, until

■ ■ ■

The next-door neighbors had a concrete goose in their front yard that they dressed up according to mood and season: a yellow slicker when it rained, a basket of colored eggs on Easter, a miniature jersey on game day. She posted about it one morning, just to let people know she was still alive, and a reporter called to interview her for the sort of feel-good story that would give people in the portal an excuse to look away from the news. "The goose is prepared for every occasion," she said grandly, pacing the smoking section in front of the hospital with a cup of coffee in her hand. "It has an outfit for every kind of day that could ever pop up on the human calendar." But when the reporter asked what she was doing in Ohio she found herself speechless, all cute little costumes of language gone, for how would you dress up a goose for this?

■ ■ ■

On the television in the NICU waiting room, a report that the dictator had finally gone too far. The next day, on the television in the NICU waiting room, a report that no he hadn't, and in fact that it was no longer possible to go too far.

■ ■ ■

A father in highly regional camouflage switched from the news to **Ancient Aliens**, where it was being posited that the metaphor of death as the Grim Reaper came from aliens in our cornfields spraying pathogens over medieval peasants. The man watched. She watched the man. Some needle in his face moved steadily from Possible, to Plausible, to I Would Die for This Belief, which was bewildering until you remembered the wild beeping of his daughter's machines.

■ ■ ■

Another baby in the NICU was named Bo, and he sobbed when he was left alone but laughed when other people came. Every day the nurses brought a mirror to Bo, and he looked into it and laughed uproariously, until it actually did start to seem funny— the unlikeliness of it all, the fact that they were all there together. Where's Bo? There's Bo. Oh there he is.

■ ■ ■

Bo's mother called his feeding tube his cheeseburgers. It was important to do things like that—if you didn't call your baby's feeding tube his cheeseburgers, then somehow the feeding tube won.

■ ■ ■

Her husband, when he flew up for a weekend visit, found himself physically incapable of being in the NICU for more than an hour. "I never realized how strong a baby's Agenda was before," he said moodily, the words STOP IT visible just near his hairline. "To make you calm, to make you feel as if nothing in the outside world is wrong. A whole room of them—well, you've got no chance."

■ ■ ■

"Ableism," her husband said, encountering this concept for the very first time. "Moby-Dick . . . was ableist . . . to Captain Ahab?"

"No," she said, her head in her hands. "No. No. No. No." His grasp of such subjects had always been limited. He believed, for instance, that sexism was when someone was "mean to Mary Tyler Moore."

■ ■ ■

"All I know is this," he told her, shifting the baby instinctively into the crook of his elbow so her oxygen levels would rise, blue as the sea, to 98 percent. "You can never call me Daddy again."

■ ■ ■

In her photoroll, between pictures of the baby appearing to smile, was a picture of perfect juggalo makeup imprinted on a woman's bare ass. "Look. Look at her beautiful face. Look how **wise**," she would tell people, total strangers, scrolling quickly past the picture of the woman's hole.

■ ■ ■

The heart grew. It hurt, where it hit the limit of the individual. It tried to follow the pathways as far as they would go. It tried not to know.

■ ■ ■

Looking at the baby she sometimes believed that nothing was wrong or could ever go wrong, that they were on a planet together where this is simply what a baby was. Then she traveled back to earth with the baby in her arms, and she gripped her stomach in pain, because suddenly the sweet small body was a jagged heap of jigsaw pieces in the bottom of her belly that she must put together, put together, keep putting together at every moment, wave after wave of that pain in the stomach, solve into a picture of the sea.

■ ■ ■

What did we have a right to expect from this life? What were the terms of the contract? What had the politician promised us? The realtor, walking us through being's beautiful house? Could we sue? We would sue! Could we blow it all open? We would blow it all open! Could we . . . could we **post** about it?

■ ■ ■

Her father holding the baby, sweating, panicked—had he ever held a baby before?—and then handing the bundle back to her after a mere five minutes. "She looks so happy in your arms," he said. "Not like mine." She knew the words that wanted to come next—**you were made for this, sweetheart, why didn't you ever**—but as a gift he did not give them to her, not this time. "Here, I'll show you what she likes," she told her father, and set her phone next to the baby's ear and played **Music for Airports**, the music streaking like a bird from one end of the terminal to the other.

■ ■ ■

"She only knows what it is to be herself," they kept repeating to each other. The rest was about them and what they thought a brain and body ought to be able to do. When the neurologist, in that first-ever meeting, had said gently that maybe the baby would one day be able to count to three, she almost turned the table over on her, because who needed to count to three? Look what counting to three had gotten us. I'm **warning** you.

. . .

"We can take her to the Cincinnati Zoo," she said, flashing on in the dark like a lightbulb. "We can put her in the double stroller, with her oxygen tank on one side, and wheel her through the crowds, and when we get to the elephant enclosure we can wrap a finger around her finger and squeeze, to show her how the little ones hold on to their mothers."

"Yes," said her sister, looking like her very young self again for a moment, and bowed her head for such a long time that it seemed she was going to cry. "We can also mourn Harambe." For whatever lives we lead they do prepare us for these moments.

. . .

The great gift of the baby knowing their voices, contentless entirely except for love—how she turned so wildly to where the pouring and continuous element was, strained her limbs toward the human sunshine, would fight her way through anything to get there.

∎ ∎ ∎

Different, yes, different. But we were going to be different, the future had asked it of us, we had already begun to change. And there was almost no human being so unlike other human beings that it did not know what a kiss was.

∎ ∎ ∎

The baby kicked her legs past other legs, punched her fists past other fists, windmilled her arms, climbed the air like a staircase. Plucked idly at the pale hair on the back of her head. It was the baby whose movements were designed for a new and unimagined landscape, the baby who was showing us how to blast off and leave—how we would fly, touch down, pick flowers in other places.

But please, not yet, we liked it here.

∎ ∎ ∎

"I want a year," her sister said fiercely. "I **want one year**," when for so long the rest of us had been thinking only how to skip ahead till the dictator was gone, how to lie down and sleep in a glass rectangle among roses till a bearable reality returned.

■ ■ ■

Her brother-in-law and sister spent late pink hours decorating the baby's nursery, though they knew she might never get a chance to sleep there. The theme they had chosen was swans, serene and graceful, though the only swan she had ever personally met had stared her down outside the Kafka Museum in Prague and then attacked. It had chased her all the way down to the water, its half-a-heart neck stretched out in a scream, but of course, she had understood later, its nest must have been somewhere near.

■ ■ ■

"If she stops breathing, it's just because she's forgotten that it's something she's supposed to do," the pregnant nurse told them, on their very last day in the NICU. "When that happens, just slap her cheeks very softly. Just give her a little pinch on the fingernail." Don't sit under the apple tree, he was the boogie woogie bugle boy of company B.

■ ■ ■

It spoke of something deep in human beings, how hard she had to pinch herself when she started thinking of it all as **a metaphor**.

■ ■ ■

They loved best to dress her precious head in pink, polka-dot, leopard-print turbans, until she looked like a psychic, until she looked like a little Golden Girl who had lived a hundred years, who stared out from underneath with the skepticism that came from having seen everything.

■ ■ ■

Instantaneous citizen of the flash of lightning that wrote across the sky **I know**.

By the time she left her sister's house, months had passed and she felt a different kind of disconnect. Dr. Butthole, for one, no longer needed her. He hid in the underside of the couch all day long, tasting himself—for even to a cat, the self was a delicacy beyond any other.

∎ ∎ ∎

"You were gone so long that Barbra Streisand became hot to me," her husband said on her return, burying his face in her neck.

∎ ∎ ∎

But he had, he informed her, **forgotten how to sleep next to another person**, and in a late-night burst of inspiration had bought himself a second bed that he placed side by side with the first. "Honey, I think you ordered the wrong size," she told him. "It looks like a baby bed." "**Not** a baby bed. Bed for an adult," he said hotly, but when she woke later and reached for him, she saw him tossing and turning in something small enough for an orphan, the blanket failing to cover him completely, his feet dangling off the flat edge of the earth.

■ ■ ■

Summer still reverberated, struck like a gong. The hot, curlicued wind carried messages to her. The whole landscape, everything she looked at, was a gold crop that needed harvesting before fall set in and the year began to see its own breath. Her arms spread wide; she felt cut open where the baby had been. Her voice, when she heard it in unguarded moments, still sounded like a flow of human sunshine, kindness. **To** somewhere.

■ ■ ■

Yet the invitations to the outside world had ceased for the moment. Schools were out and all of Europe rested and she was no longer an expert in anything, let alone what was going on.

■ ■ ■

Tatsuya Tanaka diorama of a funeral on a keyboard, miniature figures in black with their heads bowed, with a flowering wreath laid on the coffin of the plus sign.

■ ■ ■

A photo of a hot actor in a 2014 staging of **The Elephant Man**, in which he played the main role without prosthetics, just by twisting his torso and making a weird face. This was the test, she thought to herself, and waited to feel either hilarity or outrage. Neither came. He looks like he's doing a pretty good job, she decided finally. I bet his mom is proud of him, which is what she thought about most people she encountered these days.

■ ■ ■

But had she lost her ability to laugh at such things? The **New York Times** review of the play ended with this assessment of the actor's performance: "He is, as he should be, **the elephant in the room**." Ahahaha—ahahahahahahaha! No, the ability to laugh was quite intact.

■ ■ ■

She tried to reenter the portal completely, but inside it everyone was having an enormous argument about whether they had ever thought the n-word, with some people actually professing that their minds blanked it out when they encountered it in a book, and she backed out again without a sound.

■ ■ ■

The things she wanted the baby to know seemed small, so small. How it felt to go to a grocery store on vacation; to wake at three a.m. and run your whole life through your fingertips; first library card; new lipstick; a toe going numb for two months because you wore borrowed shoes to a friend's wedding; Thursday; October; "She's Like the Wind" in a dentist's office; driver's license picture where you look like a killer; getting your bathing suit back on after you go to the bathroom; touching a cymbal for sound and then touching it again for silence; playing house in the refrigerator box; letting a match burn down to the fingerprints; one hand in the Scrabble bag and then I I I O U E A; eyes racing to the end of **Villette** (skip the parts about the crétin, sweetheart); hamburger wrappers on a road trip; the twist of a heavy red apple in an orchard; word on the tip of the tongue; the portal, but just for a minute.

■ ■ ■

The flick of Joseph Campbell's too-long fingernails in **The Power of Myth**, as he speaks of the creeper that climbed the coconut tree in his house in Hawaii, how the creeper knew where to go and where to turn its leaves, how it had a form of consciousness. "I begin to feel more and more that the whole world is conscious." That "These are the eyes of the earth. And this is the voice of the earth."

■ ■ ■

If all this was thinking, then what was the head?

■ ■ ■

If you were gone from it for a little while
and then returned and no longer belonged,
what was it? A brain, a language, a place, a
time? Oh my information! Oh my everything I never knew I needed to know!

■ ■ ■

Far away now, her sister texted, I think
she's hearing rain for the very first time.
The first flake of the snow of everything,
now wild and warm. Thursday in the rain;
October in the rain; twist of a heavy red
apple; word on the tip of the tongue; grain
by green glass grain; and all of it until it
ran out.

■ ■ ■

An eye primed for reading will also read
an image—caucasianblink.gif!—so her eye
read the images her sister sent of the baby,
left to right, first toe in the bath, Russian
novels that no one would ever write,
sprawling epics that covered every inch of
the human experience, zoom in, zoom in,

zoom in. The beautiful eyes, yes, were getting bigger.

■ ■ ■

A proposed operation to stitch the baby's eyelids closed, and they suffered because so much of her communication was when her eyes widened, they believed with wonder. But on the morning of the procedure the anesthesiologist shone a light into the dolphin-blue depths, listened to the dragging tides of her breathing, and said he wouldn't, if it were his daughter he just wouldn't do it.

■ ■ ■

They dreamed, they all dreamed about her. In their dreams she crawled, ate grapes, sang nursery rhymes. In their dreams her overgrowth syndrome shot her past other people and made her powerful, and she moved among them with the use of ingenious wheels, extenders, whizbang devices. She held up her own head, she slept like other people. Above all she spoke to them, in a high-pitched otherworldly voice.

———

"I am a very advanced life-form," she announced one night, "but soon I must return . . . **to the Planet 9/11.**"

■ ■ ■

The time ripened inside gold watches. Pyramids of pumpkins and tubs of rusty orange flowers began to appear outside of grocery stores, and October issued its invitation for spirits to return to earth. In the hospital, back when they thought the baby would never leave it, her sister and her husband had gathered a pile of seasonal outfits for the baby to wear: a year in a day, winter summer spring fall.

■ ■ ■

"Can I keep you?" a woman asked her son, as she changed his diaper on a public bench. The question was monogrammed for him alone, was soft as a blanket already with use. "Can I keep you? Just for a little while?"

■ ■ ■

When it came out that we had only twelve real years left, there was a kind of urgent flowering, people everywhere felt it. Families began planning their summer trips to the Postcards, to every mountain, field, and forest on the fast-spinning rack. And novelists, in the portal, began to rise on a tide of peculiar energy. This was their moment. They were going to say goodbye to all that! They were going to say the final goodbye to all that!

∎ ∎ ∎

Meanwhile, on the earth of the baby, the climate grew hotter: icebergs melted, the seas rose, permafrost cracked to release prehistory, sections of the Great Barrier Reef blinked out whitely and one by one. Despite all this, on the earth of the baby, the thing that was people talked, touched, painted pictures, kept going.

∎ ∎ ∎

think if the ocean has a fever for years . . . lol

no sickness and broken bones

we'd be flying through the warmth more than walking

■ ■ ■

When she was fourteen weeks old they took the baby to Disney World because this, in America, was something that you did. She moved among the unknown characters serenely, she abided the fireworks, she passed through the doorways that looked like doorways and into the houses that looked like houses, only pausing to express absolute ecstasy when the band 98 Degrees began to play on the main stage at Epcot and the baby heard, she heard, her father began to dance with her, her eyes went as wide as a documentary called **Planet Earth**, cameras diving into the blue, from outer space into the deepest reefs, she fucking loves 98 Degrees, her mother exclaimed, this was the music of their youth, when the heart was a red hope, they knew every single word, the band was named for the temperature of the human

body, the baby danced, she was dancing in
her father's arms.

■ ■ ■

The baby rode with equanimity through
the darkness of the Haunted Mansion,
regarding the proceedings with the same
tolerant amusement she had shown at
her baptism. Don't worry, she seemed to
reassure her mother and father, who balanced her like a child queen between them
in their roller-coaster car: it won't be like
this, it won't be anything like this at all.
These are the **forms**, she told them earnestly, as the camera above took a picture
of them in their "corruptible mortal state,"
for everyone to laugh at together when the
ride was over. But if you ever really need it,
I will put on a white lace dress and come
to you.

■ ■ ■

A teenager on the nighttime ferry snuck his
phone over her shoulder to take pictures
of the baby in her special stroller, though

by that time it seemed baffling, she didn't look that different from other babies, did she? He was taking pictures because of her sweetness, her freshness—not because he was going to post them, right?

■ ■ ■

"I just don't want people to be scared of her," her sister had said when they first received the diagnosis, but now that the baby was here the whole family had turned to a huge blue defiant stare that moved as a part through the waves, with the fear of the world curling tall on either side of them. They wanted—what?—to take the sun by the face and force it down: Look at her! Look! Shine on her! Shine! Shine!

■ ■ ■

A round rainbow followed her on the plane ride home from Orlando. Every time she looked out the window it was there, traveling fleetly over clouds that had the same dense flocked pattern that had begun to appear on the baby's skin, the soles of her feet and palms of her hands, so she seemed to have weather for finger and footprints. The round rainbow, her answers told her when she touched down, was actually called a Glory.

■ ■ ■

Her sister painstakingly composing a letter to her senator, striking out all the phrases that looked like red meat. She wrote:

always tried to be a good citizen

ate healthy food and exercised

doctors assured us that nothing we did could have caused this

no idea when I can return to work

our insurance could drop us at any moment, due to the astronomical cost

she is the light of our lives

Asking finally, "Do you think it's too political?"

■ ■ ■

Was the baby American? If she was, was it because this was the dust that had raised her particles, was it because she was impossibly ambitious in a land of impossible ambition, or was it because this was the country that had so steadfastly refused to care for her?

The letter to the senator—begging for help, a night nurse, a day nurse, a do-over, full reproductive rights for all women, an overhaul of the entire healthcare system, a new timeline, anything, anything, everything, everything—the letter to the senator was never mailed. How could it be, when their whole clock was full of the child?

■ ■ ■

"I can do something for her," she tried to explain to her husband, when he asked why she kept flying back to Ohio on those rickety $98 flights that had recently been exposed as dangerous by **Nightline**. "A minute means something to her, more than it means to us. We don't know how long she has—I can give them to her, I can give her my minutes." Then, almost angrily, "What was I doing with them before?"

■ ■ ■

And something about the rawness of life with the baby was like the rawness of travel, the way it laid you open to the clear blue nerves. You were the five senses pouring down an unknown street; you were the slap of your shoes and hot paper of your palms, streaming past statues of regional Madonnas. The indelibility of a certain thrift shop in Helsinki, the smell of foreign decades in the lining of one leather coat. The loop of "Desert Island Disk" in a certain coffee shop in Cleveland, where the owner warned her not to have a second detoxifying charcoal latte because it would "flush the pills out of her system and get her pregnant." The bridges of other cities, where she would watch their drab green rivers buoy up their rainbow-necked ducks, where she would drink espresso until there was a free and frightening exchange between her and the day—she was open, flung open, anything could rush in.

■ ■ ■

She returned to her sister's house for the holidays. She wrestled the eighteen-pound turkey into the oven and then ran back to the couch to check the monitors. She basted it with bubbled cupfuls of white wine and then ran back to the couch to exchange the turkey's weight for the baby's. She arranged sprigs of thyme and slices of pear in champagne flutes for something called an Autumn Cocktail—she would create a holiday atmosphere or die trying! Finally, as the sun was setting, they all sat down to eat with the baby beside them, and they looked at the flowers in the center of the table, and they looked at her green grass and marigold numbers, heart rate, oxygen, and they thought of something called abundance.

■ ■ ■

Ben Franklin turkey myth: He didn't champion turkeys as nation's symbol. He used turkeys in electricity experiments

■ ■ ■

The ideal thing to watch as you held a baby having an hour-long seizure was the Hallmark Channel, which had just begun to roll out its holiday programming. The plot of a Hallmark movie, invariably, was **City Bitch Learns to Kiss a Truck . . . on Christmas**. The city bitches were exactly thirty-seven years old. Their eyes were wide with christ coke. And at the end, they were so happy to be finally taught their lesson, happy to stay in the hometowns forever, with family.

■ ■ ■

"Touch me!" the baby demanded at all times. "Touch me, I am in the dark!"

■ ■ ■

There was a robot in her sister's house that listened to them 24/7, filing their conversations away carefully in case they all murdered each other at some point. Those headlong months of words would be locked in a vault for eternity, sobbing on and on, **what will we do, what are we to do**, underpinned everywhere with the baby's breathing and the blips of her machines, occasionally brightened by her sister throwing out little interrogations of the quotidian like, **Alexa, how tall is Kevin Hart?**

Alexa, play classical music!

■ ■ ■

This time last year they had been at **The Nutcracker**, and in bed that night she closed her eyes and the ballet was still dancing itself. The ballerina was caught again and again by safe rough hands. The score filled the air like a pillow fight, but above it was the sound of toe boxes on the boards, that ugly human thump that refined the spectacle to a beauty past all bearing, so that the man in front of her broke down entirely and shouted out, "BRAVA!" Perhaps this is the afterlife, she thought, the eyes close but the ballet keeps dancing, the bodies that are the ballet still spin, as great snowy trees are lowered from the ceiling to the earth.

■ ■ ■

On Christmas Eve she took a sharp right turn and drove past the farmhouse where her great-grandmother had kept her son chained to a stake in the front yard. The shutters were a flat funeral black, like widow's weeds. The window was a merciless glass rectangle. She saw her history there as she passed, saw the circle of dead and pounded grass that was the radius of his freedom, and where he sat for hours doing the only thing he could do: see what he could see.

■ ■ ■

Movement was now completely impossible—they could no longer even take the baby in the car. Her sister's freedom had been snatched from her, neat and complete. She did not sleep or shower. Her heartbeat was the beep of the monitors. She was tied to the baby, who nevertheless had turned out to be the leafiest shade on earth, towering high above her and almost to the heavens, stirring with little birds.

■ ■ ■

To watch her sister was not like watching a saint; it was like watching the clear flowing stream the saint was filled with, water that talked, laughed, carried, lifted, and never once uttered an impatient sound. "How?" she asked her sister once, and her sister stared at her like water and said, "Perfect happiness."

■ ■ ■

God, we sound like cult members, she thought. Of course they sounded like cult members! When astrology, and crystals, and Jesus hair on dudes came back, when the apocalypse began bringing with it unbelievable sunsets, when synths appeared on the soundtrack like new kinds of hearts that might make it, when the flame leaped higher in human faces as if a gust had just come through the door, then, then! Then it was time for cults as well.

■ ■ ■

"Have you heard?" her husband cried on the phone, rattling a newspaper in the background. "Have you heard that they can now shoot a word into someone's head using a microwave ray?"

"What word?"

"Any word."

"How long does the word last?"

"We don't know yet," he told her, dropping his voice to the nightmare range. "Could be forever."

Maybe that's what happened, she thought. Maybe someone had shot the child's name into her, into some deep bull's-eye at the center of her body, maybe she would never be able to think of anything else again. Or not the name, even. Just: **Love. Love. Love.**

■ ■ ■

As the baby struggled to breathe, as it became clear that her airway was collapsing, as her head grew too heavy to even turn from side to side, it slowly dawned on them that she was experiencing an enlightenment, a golden age. She grasped beads and rattles; she answered with sweet gurgling near-giggles when you talked to her. When they played the game called Little Touch, her eyes traveled to all the places they kissed her, one by one. Against all wisdom, and in the face of her bleak gray pictures, she was learning, she could learn.

■ ■ ■

"I know when she's about to have a fit because she'll look up at something that no one else can see," a woman wrote of her daughter's epilepsy in the portal. "The other thing that will happen before her episodes—but also during and after—are her premonitions. She'll tell us something that will come true, or she'll know something she has no way of knowing." The girl had an IQ of 48, watched no television, didn't use the computer, and according to her mother could not lie.

"Epilepsy is a strange thing and I wouldn't wish it upon another person, ever. But it's made us realize that there's something special that lies in the brain. We aren't religious but it's made us believe in something unexplainable. In a way, we're grateful that some of the friends we've lost—people who couldn't cope being around it—because it's meant we've been able to have uninterrupted time with her to observe things like this." On the one hand, people who **could not be around it**. On the other hand, **things like this**.

■ ■ ■

On New Year's Eve, she leaned over the baby with a glass of champagne and sang "Bali Ha'i" right next to her ear and the baby's eyes flew wide, she went to the island. She sang "Do Re Mi" and the baby followed up and down the stairs; she sang "Over the Rainbow" and the rainbow went round.

She sang "If I Were a Bell" and that really did it; the baby pedaled her legs with excitement, she gripped her fingers with both hands, she cooed and she cooed on the same pitch, she pushed her oxygen mask away and then clutched it to her face; if I were a bell I'd go ding dong ding dong ding.

■ ■ ■

Why not, she thought, and began to read the baby Marlon Brando's Wikipedia entry. Maybe it was the champagne, but it suddenly struck her as a democratic principle, that everyone should get to know about Marlon Brando: how he looked like a wet knife in a T-shirt, the cotton ball in each cheek when he talked, rumors of him wearing diapers on the set of **Apocalypse Now**. Nothing useful, but one of the fine spendthrift privileges of being alive—wasting a cubic inch of mind and memory on the vital statistics of Marlon Brando.

■ ■ ■

Talk, laugh, carry, lift; the clear flow of animating water. Once she had flown to

New York for a photo shoot and had posed against a brick wall at golden hour wearing a large black garbage bag, but when the photographer showed her the pictures on the monitor, she was embarrassed to see that her hands were dead in every shot. The garbage bag she was swathed in had more line, more purpose—she looked like she was disappearing from a Polaroid because her parents had failed to kiss in the past. "No one knows what to do with their hands the first time," the photographer had reassured her, but now, the tension in every finger as she maneuvered the baby up the stairs; the cramps she felt in her wrists after supporting the head for an hour.

■ ■ ■

Some people were etched, transparent, lovely in their grief. But whenever she caught a glimpse of her face in the mirror behind the couch, she looked like she was trying to poop after a three-week course of Vicodin. Her stomach at all times roiled, like the comments section under a story about pillow angels.

■ ■ ■

No vehicle ever invented for the transmission of information—not the portal, not broadcast radio, not the printed word itself—was as quick, complete, or crackling as the blue koosh ball that the baby kept tucked against her chin as she slept, her small mouth open to say **oh my answers**. Her other hand she kept twisted in a bright red pom-pom, believing it was her mother's hair.

■ ■ ■

"Nobody else likes those toys," the hospice nurses told them, interested—for they, too, were gathering the pinpricks of facts that would be added to the sum total of stars in the sky. "It's too much input."

■ ■ ■

"Can she meet a dog?" she had been asking pathetically, back to the time the baby was born. "When will it be OK for her to finally meet a dog?" At last, at last, the baby got to meet a dog. It was a little white poodle, and as soon as he was set down on the couch he began to lick her all over, arms, legs, face, as if she were his long-lost owner.

"He's not allowed to be an **official** service dog," his trainer explained, "because the test is that you have to walk past a bucket of fried chicken and ignore it, and that was never gonna happen." The baby squealed and called for more. The dog ate her fingers one by one—strange, how everything in the entire world wanted to do that to a baby.

■ ■ ■

"Are you in there?" they would ask very quietly, when the baby's eyes began to travel and her heart rate climbed. When she turned lavender, blue, that quartzy gray, they all jumped up from the couch and sent their chants to her like cheer-leaders: you can do it, everybody loves you, come on come on **stay with us**.

■ ■ ■

"Keep me alive," her friend who was a disability activist had told her, and gestured toward a room of crystalline intervention: machines, tubing, oxygen. "Keep me alive till the end," she said, for she did not believe in the vegetable state. "You would come visit me, and you would read to me, and I would be in there." This belief that the I persisted, a line of light under a locked door—slim as a chance, an odd, a window, filed away fat and a little much.

■ ■ ■

The Enlightenment went on, pouring itself perpetually into the cup of coffee she drank as she watched the baby in those boiled-clear mornings. One day they had the idea to hold a toy piano up to her bare feet, and at the first note she struck she uttered a sound of wild outrage—that they had been letting her kick against air and nothingness when she could have been kicking against music this whole time.

■ ■ ■

"Write everything down," she told her sister—the portal had taught her that, that just one word could raise it all up again before your eyes—and came across a slip of paper afterward that said, "**scanning always back and forth, like someone with an endless supply of sight.**"

■ ■ ■

But she could not breathe, she gained no weight, she began to refuse the steady drip of medicines that they put into her bottle. She told them the truth, with her patient look, and so they took her to the hospital, even as they understood that the hospital meant the end. "What's wrong, honey?" one nurse asked, bending over the baby, as she opened into one of her rare high heart-tugging cries.

"Everything's wrong with her," another nurse said, almost without thinking. "With us!" she wanted to shout. Everything wrong with **us**!

■ ■ ■

Her hair had not been cut in months, and she knew the funeral might be any day, so she took an afternoon off and went to the salon. "I saw a meme the other day," her hairstylist said, concentrating hard on the back of her head. "It was about how cowlicks are formed, and it showed a cow coming into a kid's room at night and actually licking his hair, and that's how it happens."

A tear slipped from her eye in the mirror. She recalled the text thread she had going with her brother, where he just sent her minor variations of the "guess I'll die" meme, which to be honest she had never fully understood. "Oh God, did I snip you?" her stylist asked, bending down under a curtain of benevolent hair.

"No, no," she said, laying her hand on the stylist's arm, feeling that new and unstoppable stream of care pour out of her palm. "I was just thinking that you and I . . . have seen very different memes in our lives."

■ ■ ■

The next day was the baby's six-month birthday. At the last minute, the people surrounding her decided to be a party—a pink cheesecake appeared from nowhere, and a wrapped gift, and a cheerful bunch of balloons. The cake sweated silently at the end of the bed while the baby's oxygen plunged, once and then again and again. But perhaps she felt the lift of helium, sensed the sugar, perhaps the ribbon on the gift slithered and untied with every jerk of her hand, for suddenly she rallied, her breath rising with the balloons to the top of the air, and then she was awake, she was **at the party**. Visitors from miles around crowded steaming with their coats through the doorway, and everyone broke into song for her—it felt like breaking—and she smiled as she had not smiled in days. There was enough cake for everyone, and when they looked through the final smile, they saw a white glint flashing in her lower gums: first tooth, to help them eat it.

■ ■ ■

"Everyone is here," she told the baby, and then had a sudden brain wave. "**The dog is**

here," she told her, putting the limp hand up to her own short shaggy brown curls, and the baby patted back, **I know**.

■ ■ ■

Her brother leaning over the hospital bed and singing "Sunrise, Sunset" in her ear, his voice joking at first and then seamlessly serious—because she liked it, of course she liked it, she could not tell the difference between beauty and a joke.

■ ■ ■

Her face was luminous, as if someone had put flesh on the bone of the moon, and her beautiful blue eyes were larger than ever, as if coming to the end of what there was to see. This was called fluid shift, one of those accidental diamonds of hospital language that sometimes shone out from the dust. She thought of lava lamps and swallowing seas and flocks flying south, time-lapse footage of sunsets, ants clambering over molasses, the sweet spread of information, what had happened long ago, on earth and in our mouths, to the vowels. She thought of her sister in the creekbed with her body flung over her brother, protecting him from what wanted to swarm, the gold outside that wanted to swarm them till all their **in** was gone. Till they were only the movement, and the marching on.

■ ■ ■

Inside the portal, a prisoner was requesting a picture of "MOTION! I've been in solitary for 23 years & 3 days today. It's like living in a still-life painting; that's not living, it's existing; being 'in place.' So little 'moves' here. I'd like to see things moving. Perhaps traffic at night, lights shining & the trails from lights whizzing past. Or water flowing from a stream, waterfall etc. that shows motion. Or snow while it is falling? Anything in MOTION!" Outside the window, the request whirled down, each flake the first flake, first flake of the snow of everything.

■ ■ ■

The day after the birthday party the hospital room was dark. It smelled of human milk and store-bought cookies and top-of-the-head sweetness. Everyone else had gone out to breakfast, and her sister had fallen into a near-unconscious sleep on the couch in the corner. She curled up in the hospital bed next to the baby. She held the little hand and waited for its wilted pink squeeze, like the handshake of a lily. She stroked the heaving back—how hard it was, to haul the body through even a single day—and traced the new brown down on the baby's forehead. She leaned over the child and said something; she said, "It is going to be just like your mother." The moment was so pristine and so meaningful that something must be done to alleviate it, so she picked up her phone and began scrolling through Jason Momoa pics, all the while thinking, bitch, if this even happens while you were looking at Jason Momoa pics?!?

■ ■ ■

A nurse turned the baby on her back and shone a strong light into her eyes, so that afterward they would always wonder if the light itself had done it, opened an elevator door and let her on. The oxygen levels on the monitor began to fall, and everyone crowded into the room. Music, her sister called, and she flapped her hands, frantic, what do you play? What do you play as someone is dying? A name flashed into her mind—perhaps because she saw the cracked cassette case on the floor of her mother's van, perhaps because those **Pure Moods** commercials were stamped on her memory along with the imagery of ocean waves, perhaps because she had recently read a thinkpiece about her unexpected critical resurgence—the name that flashed into her mind was Enya.

■ ■ ■

Six months and one day old. Everything contained in that extra day, that overflow. It was not frightening, nothing was frightening. The nurses lifted her up so her parents could hold her again. Her head tilted back and her mouth opened as if to drink; her lips turned the gentle color of fingertips in winter. All of them gathered around her and poured out spontaneous speeches as they gripped her hands, feet, ankles. What they repeated, oddly enough and over and over, was that she had done a good job.

The nurses gave her morphine and Ativan through a port in her pink heel—like mythology, as if she were immortal in every other part of her. Hic, hic, hic, the baby said, the faint voltage of **I am** ran and kept running as long as it could. "Such a good job," they all said till the end.

■ ■ ■

It was like nothing any of them had ever seen. There was nothing trivial left in the room—not the clearing of a throat, not an itch on the arch of a foot—except that phone on the pillow, which had malfunctioned somehow to keep playing "Sail away, sail away, sail away."

■ ■ ■

Her mother and father cut the top two locks of hair off her head, the ones that curled mischievously to either side like that gif of the grinch.

■ ■ ■

Their mother changed the baby's diaper, and there was present in her hands a thousand diaper changes leading up to the perfection of one. The priest had come earlier, with the whole Mass packed into a little suitcase that was branded **Rome Essentials**, but this was the act that broke into the temple and drank up the holy wine, this was the gesture that entered into gold. Every joke she had ever told about diapers vanished up into the air like an incense.

■ ■ ■

Two nurses gave her a sponge bath, crooning to her as if she were still alive. "You're so good," the nurses said. "You're being so good, sweetheart. Now just turn over and we'll get your back." Finally they each slid a hand under her neck and lifted and there she was, her knowledge finally unheavy, staring straight up at the ceiling for the first time. Holding up her head! they all exclaimed. Sleeping like other people!

■ ■ ■

She sang into the cup of the baby's ear as she was being washed, for her hearing hung perceptibly above them, like a big bronze bell now rocked to a stop. Strange, but she couldn't seem to remember anything but the most universal choruses, jukebox hits, stadium anthems—songs where the radio rested after scanning past the shouting evangelists, where the whole family lifted up together and let whatever the human voice was just fly.

■ ■ ■

The baby did not ever lose her warmth, as long as she was in that room. Their father would carry her down to the morgue himself, breaking all the rules, insisting, **let me**, with a blanket so she would not be cold, and his own pearl-gray rosary wrapped around her wrist.

■ ■ ■

An hour went missing while she wandered the halls with the family's belongings piled on a hotel cart, and then one of the nurses who had given the baby a sponge bath was holding her next to the hospital entrance, saying the words "Your singing . . ." into her ear. She concentrated on a patch of empty air behind the nurse's shoulder, for she knew if she turned her head even one degree she would see herself on the phone in the smoking section, holding a cup of coffee and being interviewed about the concrete goose, which was wearing black today.

■ ■ ■

The end of the Wikipedia entry always the most suspect. But listen, this time it was true.

■ ■ ■

The light on the drive home was like the hide of a breathing animal, silver and gold hillsides of it, fawn and rabbit and fox quivering in a blue snow. It allowed her to approach even though she was human; for once it was not afraid. Under the echoing dome she kept hearing the disembodied cry, "But she's not **gone**, is she? She can't be **gone**?" Then the nameless birds were caught and lifted until they were just the light on their undersides.

■ ■ ■

At the Cloisters, she remembered, pressing her flaming cheek against the window, thinking of the rosary wound round the little wrist, one of the wooden statues was alive. The forehead leaped out of itself and into the real world; it bulged with one ripe thought, which was the resurrection of the body. It was Jesus, and perhaps he really had been raised, for the sign that was nailed up next to him said, **The fingers on his right hand have been restored**.

■ ■ ■

Like hey! More legs!

■ ■ ■

They did not, in the immediate aftermath, holding heaps of downy garments on their laps, wish for a cure. They wished for a better way to preserve a human smell. She and her mother and sister tore through the house like gray calligraphic hounds on a scent, and when they found a onesie or pair of socks or little tutu that was marked with that glowing signature they waved it in the air and said, "Here!"

■ ■ ■

She put on a T-shirt that was stained with the baby's eyedrops and tucked the koosh ball under her pillow. She set her 24-hour NICU badge on the nightstand and told herself that if the volcano erupted at midnight, it would find her with all the right things surrounding her, so bring on the black ash, she said, and slept.

■ ■ ■

At the funeral home, as the family sat down for a meeting with the funeral director, her brother fucked up and somehow introduced himself as the baby's **husband**. Their laughter approached hysteria, tears streaked down their faces, they gripped each other's arms and could not stop. She closed her eyes against her brother's shoulder and saw him carrying the baby into the woods, where his green skills waited to keep them all safe.

■ ■ ■

"That one," her sister told the undertaker, and pointed to a casket sunk deep with pillowy satin, an open valentine that even in the picture seemed to lower itself perpetually into a white ground. Something of her old voice returned to her here, the one that stamped her **born in 1987** and that had seemed so in danger of disappearing. "That one right there. Because she classy."

■ ■ ■

After the meeting, she wandered through what looked like a gift shop, full of brass urns and memorial collages, pocket watches and Swarovski roses, granite slabs sandblasted with the faces of bygone Lindas. She lingered there for a considerable time, picking up paperweights and setting them down, for she only ever liked to travel when she got a souvenir. did you know you can get your ashes put into a golf ball? she texted a friend. did you know that your casket can be camouflage? did you know they can put you in a papier-mâché turtle and release you into the sea?

it me

■ ■ ■

Man, it's a hot one

started to flicker out of the radio as they were driving home, and her father and brother-in-law began, in sweet fraternity, to extol the virtues of Carlos Santana's guitar playing, which they could only describe as being out of this world.

**My muñequita
my Spanish Harlem
Mona Lisa**

A dead reflex kicked in her throat. Had she ever found that funny? Or had the laughter waited, external, for her to give in and join it?

■ ■ ■

At the nail salon, the technician introduced himself as Google. "Because I know everything," he said. He smiled against a blinding wall of every imaginable color, a hand with a thousand fingertips, heaven, and asked if they were going to a party. She whispered to him the truth and Google crossed himself; now he knew one more thing. "I'll do glow-in-the-dark, OK?" he said, and began buffing the nails with infinite gentleness. "Go into the dark later and you'll see them, every one."

■ ■ ■

The Men's Wearhouse where the boys were measured for their suits was holy; the T.J. Maxx where the girls texted each other pictures from their respective dressing rooms was holy; the Shoe Carnival where they staggered up and down the aisles almost laughing; the Michael's where they chose posterboards for collages; the florist where they pointed at baby's breath; the bakery where they deliberated over tea cookies; the Clinique counter where they bought waterproof mascara; the Cheesecake Factory where they ate bang-bang shrimp after it all and were very very kind to each other was holy, and the light fixtures she always made fun of seemed to bloom the whole time on their stems.

■ ■ ■

The dog who had met and kissed the baby came to the nighttime visitation and lapped at the long line of mourners as they blew through the door. "Animals are allowed?" she asked the funeral director. "Animals are allowed," he said, and told her that once a horse had come, and was led up the aisle so he could nuzzle his owner for the last time, seeking among her face for sugar cubes, breathing the just-cut hay of her hair, still feeling in his body the hot red Yes that jumped to her smallest commands. But "Let me go" was now the order, and what the body said was No.

■ ■ ■

The dog was lowered to the baby in her casket and greeted her with visible recognition. Everyone wept at this, for she was still as a peach in a painting, and she wore an opaque mask of makeup and was no longer warm. Her eyes had been glued shut, and her hands no longer commanded the air, and her squeal had been returned to sound itself—so what was it about her that he recognized, what was it about her that the little dog still loved? Yet he did. He scrambled among the valentine satin and tried to wash her face back to what he knew.

■ ■ ■

I am I because my little dog knows me— who said that? She swore she had seen it somewhere in the portal, painted on a piece of plywood and hanging in someone's home. As the wake murmured on around her, she climbed up bodily on the banister that separated the dead from the living and sat there, letting the line multiply behind her, leaning close to the child's ear to tell her goodbye, I am I because my little dog knows me.

■ ■ ■

The neurologist showed up toward the end, and she found herself asking why she **had** gone into that green growing field, why she had chosen to study the human brain in the first place. The choice glowed with greater meaning, as the starlike tracheotomy scar on the throat of the respiratory therapist had glowed. "That's a very long story that I'll tell you someday," the woman smiled, so that she saw her standing barefoot in the branches of her own family tree, white asterisks on the shoulders of her black wool coat.

■ ■ ■

To be a member of a generation meant that her sister put on a hot pink dress for the funeral, chose lipstick and towering high heels to match, all the while yelling, "WE GOTTA LOOK GOOD FOR OUR BABY!" To be a member of a generation meant that the casket was pink too, a new shade of pink just recently named, that someone snuck a bright clear amethyst into it before it was closed. That the hour she was buried was dark inside the day, and rain fell in its great gray population; that the whole family gathered outside, which still existed, and stood under an evergreen tree. That trap music was played at the wake, that afterward they ate barbecue, that her brother slapped his chest and told his sister, "Girl, she was a real one." So specificity was present as a living thing, a guest.

■ ■ ■

At the wake, she and her sister held some-one else's newborn, and the little bundle was so light and uncomplicated that they kept resisting an urge to toss her up to the ceiling and catch her, for they knew she would always return to them. "She's like another species," her sister said softly, young and lovely in her hot pink dress, her arms weighed down by hardly more than a feather.

■ ■ ■

They came home and her brother-in-law knelt down and kissed it, the square of the couch where she had lived, where she had lain among machines, where they had discovered, almost too late, that they could play patty-cake with her.

■ ■ ■

The koosh ball was accidentally thrown away, and little did the landfill know what was coming: the blue bursting star of everything she knew, never smaller by one ray.

■ ■ ■

There began a period where she cried uncontrollably in cafés, taxis, grocery stores, bars; at commercials, at documentaries, at Ryan Reynolds movies; in public bathrooms, with her head on her knees, making animal noises that could not belong to her; when the FedEx woman called her sweetheart; when her sister said, "You were her mother too"; in the portal, where the entirety of human experience seemed to be represented, and never the shining difference of that face, those eyes, that hair.

■ ■ ■

Would it change her? Back in her childhood she used to have holy feelings, knifelike flashes that laid the earth open like a blue watermelon, when the sun came down to her like an elevator she was sure she could step inside and be lifted up, up, past all bad luck, past every skipped thirteenth floor in every building human beings had ever built. She would have these holy days and walk home from school and think, After this I will be able to be nice to my mother, but she never ever was. After this I will be able to talk only about what matters, life and death and what comes after, but still she went on about the weather.

■ ■ ■

Night after night afterward, with her finger-nails glowing in the dark, she dreamed that the baby was still doing a kind of tiny breathing that they had somehow over-looked. Someone always yelled, "HEY!" and the funeral was called off right in the middle. They lifted her from her casket and kissed her; they pelted pink carnations out the window of the car as they drove home; it had all been a mistake. They had only had to notice something smaller than before.

■ ■ ■

The doors of bland suburban houses now looked possible, outlined, pulsing—for behind any one of them could be hidden a bright and private glory. The woman who had once been called the voice of God, who had been absent from the stage for two decades, went on singing in her own home, her partner heard her. He felt sorry for the rest of the world, he said.

"I just had a lot of something—what was it?" the singer had once told an interviewer. "So much sun, I suppose, running through me. All this wonderful sun!" The doors of suburban houses might be shut up on that sun.

■ ■ ■

The doctors had asked for the brain, with so much hope that it was almost tender, as if they loved her too. "Do you think she would mind?" her sister had asked, and she pressed the heels of her hands against her eyes and saw rockets shoot across that internal black dome. "No, I don't think she would mind at all," she had responded, and now that the act was accomplished, it gave comfort: as long as people were looking at that mind, it was still active in the world, asking and answering, finding out about things, making small dear cries of discovery. It had, the doctors confirmed, only ever kept growing while she was alive.

■ ■ ■

Keep reading a little longer, not totally against your will.

■ ■ ■

"My battery is low and it is getting dark," the Mars Rover said in the portal.

■ ■ ■

The film waited for her to watch it, glowing black and white at the center of her collection. One afternoon when her husband was away she put it on and saw Anthony Hopkins' face shining in the dark as he beholds the Elephant Man for the first time, all beauty breaking in on him, his left eye askew like a dried violet. What she had not expected to feel was simple happiness, as she looked at the layers of makeup and the bulbous prosthetics, as if her extraordinary companion were back with her again and the room brimful of her breathing. When the Elephant Man finally speaks, it is like her dreams of the baby: he opens his mouth and the Bible comes out, Shakespeare, Milton, the poets. The doctors burst in on him just as he finishes the psalm. "All the days of my life," he says, standing tall, "and I will dwell in the house of the Lord for ever."

■ ■ ■

Where was that house, where did we go on and on in the long word **dwell**? In the portal, a call for Joseph Merrick's bones to be finally laid to rest, though his family had given him wholly to science.

■ ■ ■

In the portal, a picture of Joseph Merrick's skull, where on the right side the bone grew fractally, like cave or crystal or ivy, hand over hand and almost flowing. It did not look strange. It looked, when all was said and done, like what a skull wanted to do.

■ ■ ■

The minor physical adjustments she had once habitually made—lifting her breasts toward her collarbone whenever she looked in the bathroom mirror, snipping the ends off stray curls before she went to parties— had flown from her, had perhaps gone wherever the baby had gone. She now took perverse pleasure in the fact that the last time she had looked nice was on the leather couch at that Disney World hotel, basking in a clarified light, every laugh line visible, cradling the darling's head between two breasts that felt like clouds. And sun running through her, sun, wonderful sun.

■ ■ ■

"I would have done it for a million years," her sister said, toneless. "I would have gotten up every morning and given her thirteen medicines. There is no relief. I would have done it for all time." Then told of a bill she had received for $61,000. Then sent a picture of a vial of snow a nurse had gathered from that night, clear liquid asterisks, **her** snow.

■ ■ ■

Her sister's husband went to a garage sale one afternoon and purchased like fifty Beanie Babies. This, too, was one of the remedies for grief. Someone had sat them on little stools in their display cases, so they would not get tired—of what?—of the long direct daylight of being Beanie Babies. Someone had cared for them. Perhaps everyone was a god with their eye on some small sparrow. Perhaps everyone was the collector of some soft rare commemorative, stitched with a visible heart and worth millions on millions in the mind.

■ ■ ■

RELATED SEARCHES

i miss my son who died

i miss my son so much quotes

i miss my son in heaven

my son died and i miss him

missing my son sayings

■ ■ ■

At a meeting to discuss the autopsy results, the doctor took a bite of bagel and
shaped with his mouth the great word **why**.
"When Jesus met the blind man, his dis-
ciples asked him why—was it the man's sin,
was it the sin of his parents? And Jesus said
it was no one's sin, that it happened so that
God might move us forward, through and
with and in that man." Tears stood without
falling in the doctor's blue eyes; that is the
medicine, she thought. "If I can do anything . . ." he said chokingly, with a slight
amount of cream cheese in his mustache,

which increased her love for the human race, which moved her forward through, with, in him, which was also for the glory of mankind.

■ ■ ■

"Why was she able to do what she could do?" they asked the doctors. "How could she breathe on her own, breastfeed, answer when we talked to her?" The doctors did not know. They spoke of the brain's enormous plasticity. Yes, she felt that, she held it in her hand. She remembered pressing warm Silly Putty against newspaper until it picked up a whole paragraph of what was happening, clear enough to read. Then folding and folding it to blankness again.

■ ■ ■

"Can ghosts learn new technology?" her sister asked, thinking of what must come next, the endless conveyor of progress to which a whole human history's worth of spirits must adapt. The two of them were silent for a minute, and then images came crowding in: an elevator ghost pressing every button, feeling its stomach drop out through the bottom of the world; a ghost unzipping its message across long black telegraph wires; ghosts in the portal, reading forever, tenderly holding down hearts. In the group text where they sent her videos back and forth late at night, that's what they said—thank God, can you believe, that we had the technology.

■ ■ ■

What if that teenage boy **had** put her in the portal? It was hard to imagine a time when that would have made her angry. She would be so grateful, now, to have people meet the baby in the broad electric stream of things—to know a picture of her, blurred, in motion, was living its own life far from actual fate, in the place where images dwelled and dwelled.

■ ■ ■

"Her grass looks great," her sister said, sending a picture of the rampantly growing grave—the green real park they had walked through day by day while she was with them, for there are people in this life we are assigned to watch over. Her sister snipped blades of it and mailed them to her, to carry with her on her travels. She saw a wild un-domestic blanket of it growing in profusion over abandoned suburbs and cities, over the places where we all used to live.

■ ■ ■

Surrounding the meticulous documenta-tion of the baby's final days in her photoroll were: a picture of Ray Liotta's recent plastic surgery; a screenshot of a news story about how fake nudes of a congresswoman had been debunked by foot fetishists; a blonde Fox News anchor with a graphic next to her reading THE HAT THAT DARE NOT SHOW ITS BRIM; a fluffy eagle with black wings and filmy gray eyes that, as her friends had spent one marvelous free field day pointing out, looked like it knew the exact hour when you would die; and min-utes before it happened, herself, bent over in the darkness of that hospital room and wearing sailor stripes. It would show up on her screen in another year, the announcement that she had a new memory.

■ ■ ■

scanning back and forth

an endless supply of sight

■ ■ ■

Gradually the world called her back. As her plane dragged its dotted line across the Atlantic, she looked out the window again and saw the same Glory following her, a round blaze of rain that never blinked.

Her eyes floated two inches in front of her and seemed to be raining too. The book she had brought, with its soft-focus woman on the cover, lay untouched on her lap. She began to flip through the pictures again: the baby smiling, laughing, at a pumpkin patch, in a bathing suit being dipped in the ocean. The pictures were always with her; she could not feel her first fingertip. Once, she had visited a little island with shocking white beaches and had worked her bare toes into its famous sand, which was used to make the glass for all our screens. There the sky was so crystal, and the sun so hot, and the air on her skin so unmediated, and the trees so full of koala bears, that she felt either like she had gotten inside the phone completely or else had gotten out.

■ ■ ■

Piles of discarded devices in landfills, with somewhere among them a koosh ball still flickering, trying to transmit—**do you copy, do you copy, do you read, do you read**. "I copy," she said to the vibrating air, "I copy, I copy, I read."

■ ■ ■

She had been asked to give a lecture at the British Museum. The lecture was about the portal, and as she stood at the podium and clicked through the PowerPoint she tried to pretend she still lived there, that still she pumped with the blood that knew. She said the words **communal mind** and saw the room her family had sat in together, looking at that singular gray brain on an MRI. She thought about the 24-hour NICU badge in her coat pocket, that she kept there to remind herself she had once been a citizen of necessity. Why had she entered the portal in the first place? Because she wanted to be a creature of pure call and response: she wanted to delight and to be delighted. She read, her rib cage shaking, with the voice she had used to delight the baby. Her heart hammered nearly out of her and she read:

"She was asked to give a lecture at the British Museum. This was hardly deserved. She had, in a sense, stolen her way there, bit by bit, scroll by scroll, gold piece by gold piece. Still, she stood there, and locked them in her mind for an hour. Her face was the fresh imprint of her age. She spoke the words that were there for her to speak; she wore the only kind of shirt available at that time. It was not possible to see where she had gone wrong, where she would go wrong. She said **garfield is a body-positivity icon**. She said **abraham lincoln**

is daddy. She said **the eels in London are on cocaine**. It was fitting finally to appear in that place, an exhibit herself and from far away, collaged together in body and mind, monstrous in the eyes of the future, an imbecile before the Rosetta Stone, disturber of the deadest tombs, butterfly catcher and butterfly killer, soon to be folded between two pages herself, and speak about the liftedness of little and large things."

The audience was silent, and the faces in the front row were shining. This did not feel like real life exactly, but nowadays what did. What she was imagining was carrying the baby through the museum, the head in her arms unheavy. She was showing her the mummies, setting her lightly down on the steps of the temple, calling her name to the echoing ceiling, carrying her through the Greek marbles and saying, "Someone in some future time will think of us." She was cracking open the glass case of amulets and hanging every limb of her with protection, protection. She was standing in the hall of the Assyrian lions and assuring her that we would not be devoured, she was carrying her, carrying her, stopping at every fountain and letting her drink, from prehistory to the modern age, to the moment of them standing there together, marveling: more and more I begin to feel that the whole world is conscious.

■ ■ ■

Afterward, and after many drinks, people from the audience led her down winding side streets to a club with no name. The club was a crush, one body. A mirror at the back that she first thought was another room, until she saw her own face at the center of it. A sign on the wall that said OASIS. At first she could not dance at all, and then she could not stop. The songs they played were preposterous; were her personal American embarrassments; the ones that had marked her as backward, provincial, unsubtle as a major chord. They played "Rock and Roll All Nite." They played "Seven Nation Army." They thumped up and down like Ohioans to "Sweet Caroline." Oh, she said to herself, I did not know. The songs all along had been beloved. The whole club pressed against her and she thought of Little Touch; her eyes traveled to all the places she was kissed, places all over the world. She wondered was it worth it to show up, hear a little music, and then leave? Someone at some point slid her phone out of her pocket and she lifted off her feet, lighter. Her whole self was on it, if anyone wanted. Someone would try to unlock it later, and see the picture of the baby opening her mouth, about to speak, about to say anything.

Acknowledgments

My thanks to my editor, Paul Slovak, who accompanied me on this journey despite not knowing what a binch is, and to my agent, Mollie Glick, who first found me in the portal. Thanks also to the team at Riverhead: Alexis Farabaugh, Helen Yentus, Jynne Dilling Martin, May-Zhee Lim. And in memory of Liz Hohenadel and her long crisp gingerish hair.

To everyone who read early drafts: Greg, Michelle, Jami, Maryann, Sheila. To Jason, who read a thousand incarnations of this, including one in which the husband character belonged to an underground anarchist collective called My Cummies.

To the people I have met around the world who showed up here as photographs, cartoons, and phantoms. I am writing this in quarantine; I miss you all. And to the other members of the communal mind.

My thanks to the **London Review of**

Books and the British Museum, who allowed me to give an excerpt of this in 2019 as the least educational lecture ever delivered in those halls. And to my compatriots at the Spanish Bar.

To the doctors, especially Dr. Habli, Dr. Smith, and Dr. Vawter-Lee. To the NICU nurses, especially Janet, who showed us how to hold her. And to the StarShine workers, who brought boxes of toys.

More information about Proteus Syndrome can be found at https://www.proteus-syndrome.org. Donations to that organization go toward research and helping to network people living with Proteus Syndrome, most of them children and teenagers.

Donations can also be made to Pets for Patients (https://www.petsforpatients.org), an organization that matches pets with the families of chronically and terminally ill children.

To my sister and my brother-in-law, who let me share in her life. And most of all to my little love Lena. You were not here to teach us, but we did learn.

PATRICIA LOCKWOOD was born in Fort Wayne, Indiana, and raised in all the worst cities of the Midwest. She is the author of two poetry collections, **Balloon Pop Outlaw Black** and **Motherland Fatherland Homelandsexuals**, and the memoir **Priestdaddy**, which was named one of the ten best books of 2017 by **The New York Times Book Review**. Lockwood's writing has appeared in **The New York Times**, **The New Yorker**, **The New Republic**, and the **London Review of Books**, where she is a contributing editor.

Find her on Twitter at @TriciaLockwood.

P.O. 0005026605 20210339